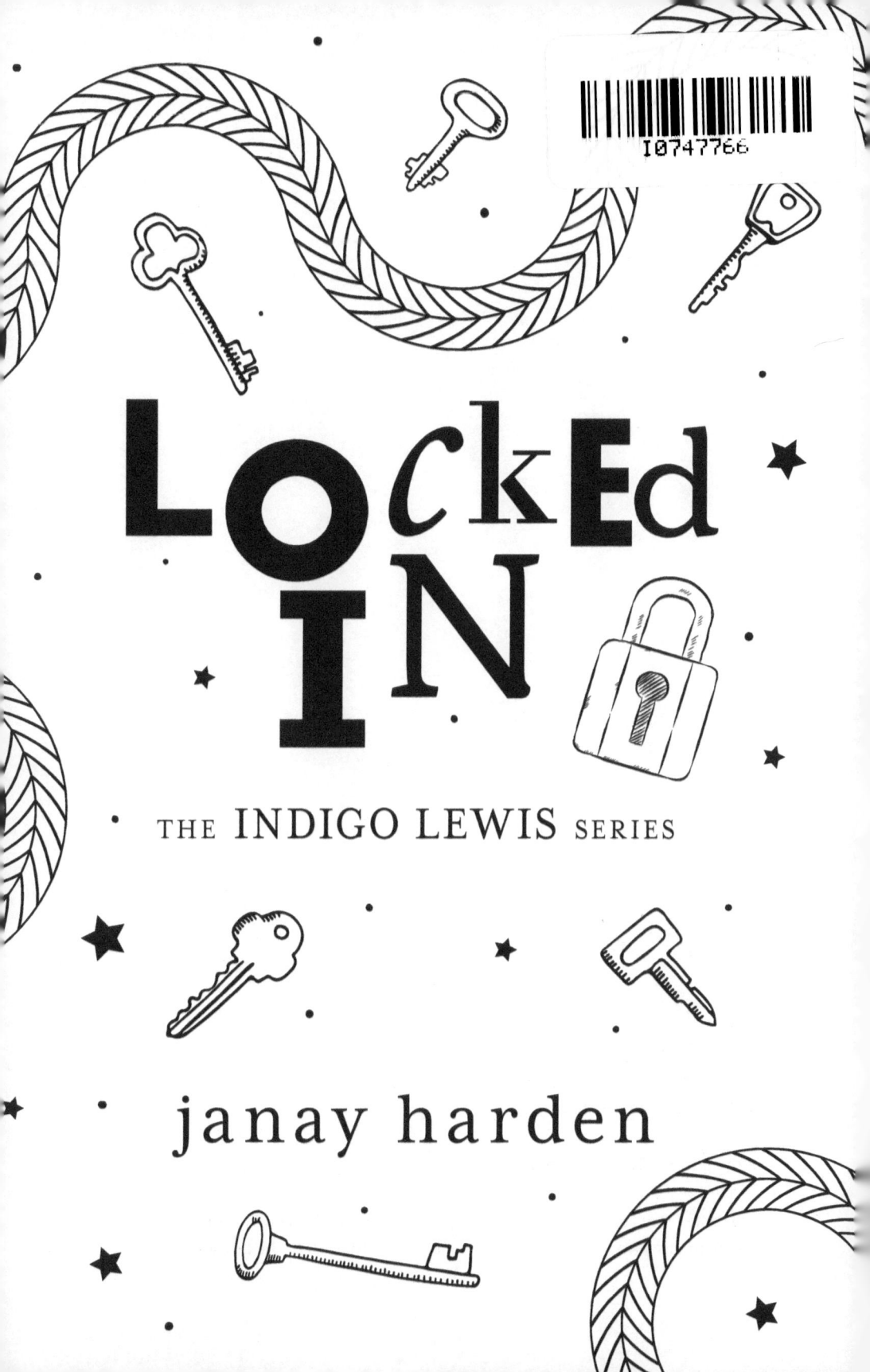

LOckEd IN

THE INDIGO LEWIS SERIES

janay harden

Locked In
The Indigo Lewis Series

Copyright © 2022 by Janay Harden

Thank you to everyone and everything that shook me up
and pushed me out of my comfort zone.

The world needs more shaken up women.

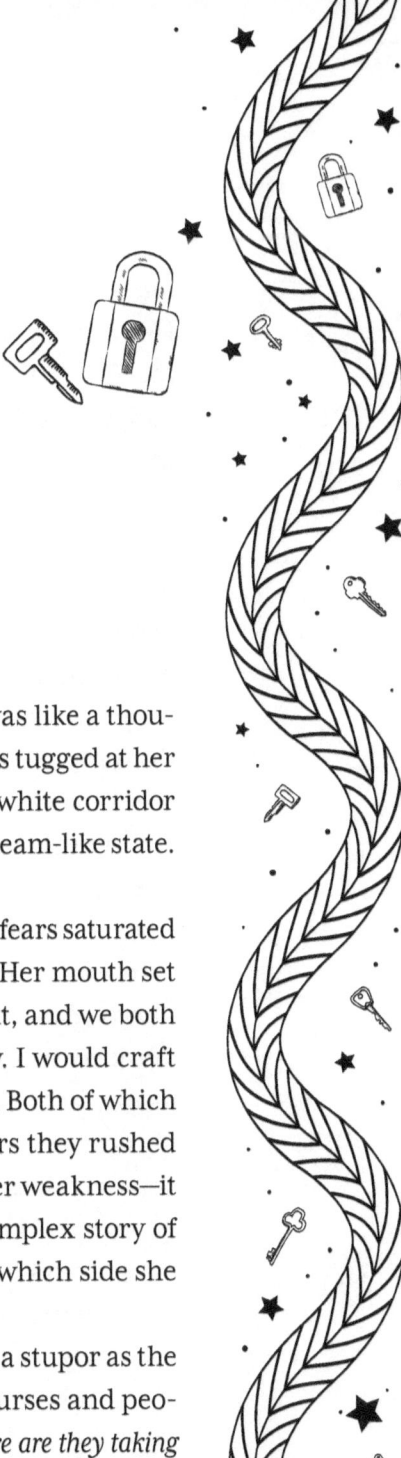

PROLOGUE

WATCHING HER BEING dragged away was like a thousand bee stings to my heart. The nurses tugged at her arms and guided her down the long, white corridor into nothing-land. She looked comatose. In a dream-like state. Only this wasn't a dream.

Her face was hard. Mine was wet. My deepest fears saturated my t-shirt on display and for everyone to see. Her mouth set in a straight line. One day, if things worked out, and we both made it out of this alive; I would tell her story. I would craft beautiful words to describe her love and pain. Both of which crashed together like the square hospital doors they rushed her through. Mental illness had never been her weakness—it had always been her superpower. It was a complex story of saints and villains, and I didn't always know which side she fell on. Maybe that's how she preferred it.

With widened and empty eyes, she stood in a stupor as the doors swung back and forth surrounded by nurses and people in white coats. They buzzed around. *Where are they taking her? What will they do to her? Do they think she's a black woman in her fifties, having a mental health crisis?* But they didn't know her. Shit, I hardly did.

1

They tugged at her arms and shooed her along, but her feet were cemented firmly on the linoleum tile that hospitals were famous for. Those dark eyes studied my face—so similar to hers. Her chest rose up and down, and calmness swept over her that I didn't recognize. The halls were bare and white. They had no love. No colors of red for fiery passion. No yellow hues for hope. None of it looked inviting, and it made my stomach churn to think about the things they would do to her. If this was a safe place—I didn't feel it. So many unspoken words passed between us. Baskets filled with yesterday's memories and the future that probably would never happen. I told her my deepest, darkest secrets in my moments of despair and when she looked at me right now—I wondered if she was thinking about them? Whispers I told her in the night. Were they replaying like scenes from a movie in her brain like they did in mine?

We trimmed her hair short, and the tips were dirty blonde from the rushed cut and dye job we did back in the motel's bathroom. She was technically on the run. I mean, how else did you describe an escape from a mental institution? It was lopsided and jagged at the ends, but it framed her syrupy, brown face and molded her rounded jaw. My Mona Lisa held my heart and mind captive. A light sheen sat on her forehead, and I could tell from here her nose was sweating. *'Your nose only sweats if you're mean,'* Grandpa Ez used to say. That was before the police killed him. They had described him as aggressive, intimidating even. He was none of those things. Grandpa Ez was our glue and with him gone, life was not normal. None of this was, and that's why I had to be the one to put us back together.

It took us two weeks to get to know each other and peel back layers of an onion we hid from the world. We laughed and cried. We ate and we argued. She ripped my emotional

bandages off and never prepared me for the truth scabs that would surely form.

I wished to God she was different.

She held me as I cried. When I grumbled about all the things wrong with my life, she wiped my face and showed me the beauty of finding myself. Even when I didn't want her to, she knew me better than most. And I had repaid her by bringing her *here*.

They yanked at her arm once more, but this time with more force as two muscular, fat head security guards were chomping at the bit itching to be called in. She blinked and ended our locked trance before she went back into character. With perfect teeth and a dazzling smile, she spun around and pushed the nurses against the walls, demanding to walk by herself. Her floor-length, wool petticoat caught a breeze and dangled in the wind behind her. Her head was high, and nose was in the air when she sauntered past staff, giving them the middle finger along the way.

Then she was gone.

I leaned against the wall right under a bright red EMERGEN-CY sign, and my body felt punctured while the bees attacked my heart again. People typically came to the hospital when they were in distress or needing medical attention. She didn't need serious medical attention, but she *was* in distress. The distress was in her mind, and it was something that would cost me a sum too great.

She was a murderer.

So was I.

She had killed a man simply for the fun of it.

So had I.

Some called her Sonia. Some called her crazy. Some called her a killer.

I just called her Mom.

3

PART 1
MEMORIES

CHAPTER ONE

"**Y**OU SAID YOU were a writer, right?" Kathleen ogled me and held the door open I just buzzed. I recognized her name as my teammate from all the emails we exchanged the past few weeks.

"Yes. I'm Indigo Lewis. You can call me Indy."

Kathleen's hair fell just right at her shoulders and I was jealous since I chopped off all my hair when Ez passed. Hers framed her face in such a way that made me hopeful that she and I wouldn't have to be the token Black girls of the team. I looked around at pale faces and guesstimated that it was her and I that would be the coffee to this milk. There were droves of seasoned writers and four interns hired total, and even though I had first dibs on all the best assignments—per the welcome email, first day jitters had me by the balls.

"I'll walk you to the back where everyone else is."

"Everyone else?" I repeated. "Am I late or something?"

Kathleen bit her lip. "Did you get the email? Start time changed to 8:30 a.m., not 9 a.m. anymore. Something about union lunches."

I gritted my teeth. I was late for day one of my internship. "Who emailed?"

"Ms. O'Sullivan. . ." Kathleen's voice trailed off.

Harper. I dropped my chin. Harper.

Day one at Synergy Publishing House and News, as a new intern, was off to a great start. I glanced over Kathleen's shoulder, searching for my supervisor, Harper O'Sullivan.

After they killed Ez, I spent months back home in Tunica Rivers. My dad, my sister; Sidney, and my dad's girlfriend, Ms. Arletha, were in a daze following the loss of him, and everyone operated in a fog, clouded by their own self-imposed guilt.

I wrote, cried, and ate. It was weird. When I was in high school, writing came easily to me. The words flowed straight from my brain to the pen. Away at college, I hardly did any creative writing—there were crickets in my brain, and I could barely formulate syllables. When I went home and sat at the water for days, the words came back. I filled up notebook after notebook as stories and letters to Mom and Ez poured from my heart. It brought the sun back. It brought me back.

Harper was my old work-mom from the theater where I had my work-study gig last year. I spent many late nights in the theater reading her different things I had written, and she always said I didn't take myself seriously. Harper listened on the phone many nights as I cried and read her poems about Ez. Well, as luck would have it, she got this supervisor position on the outskirts of campus. She called me up and hollered into the phone, *'Indy pack your bags, Head Girl! We're heading to the big leagues.'* I almost peed my pants when she called! I packed my bags and headed back to school to start the Fall semester, lugging dozens of loose-leaf pages, pens, and highlighters. I had to hold everyone in my family together and the only way I knew how to do that was to get an education and get us out of Tunica Rivers where we had lost too much.

Head Girl, she called me. She said I was always somewhere with my head in the clouds. When you had voices that festered inside of you no matter how hard you tried to tame them, living in your head didn't seem so bad. But I digress.

Don't go being mean to yourself! I knew Ez would squabble.

The same day the police murdered Ez died, my boyfriend, Chaquille, had a Grand Mal seizure, which left him in need of physical therapy for months. He had trouble walking and standing for long periods of time. It scared me. We almost lost him; just like my Ez. Imagine; loving Ez all nineteen years of my life and trying to figure out if I loved Chaquille too—only to lose the only one I was *sure* about. Losing Ez was like not being able to breathe. A pain sat in the middle of my chest that just would not go away. The pressure sat there and if I inhaled too hard; I was sure it might pop. After him and Chaquille, that's when the pain in my chest started. *I feel myself breathing, but I'm not breathing.*

After dropping Chaquille at physical therapy this morning, his face was so clear and his eyes strong. We were kinda sorta living together, but not really because it wasn't sanctioned by the university. When I told him I was back in town, he showed up and never left. I had showered and scrubbed the remnants of a night with him off my body. His fingerprints were still visible on my skin, and that made me smile. Chaquille could throw down in the bedroom. I wondered how his day was going.

While grieving Ez, the Fall semester crept up and right on past me, and so when Harper called, I had already missed a few weeks of class, but the internship was just starting today. Thank God. I needed to graduate on time and this internship was my fresh start. With Chaquille and Harper by my side, I was going to write my ass off this year. I had to make it count and get out of my own way.

When I tuned back to Kathleen, she was still talking. "No worries, we're not really doing anything right now." Kathleen

waved me away, sensing my growing worry. The inside of the hallway was long and bright. Pictures of Louisiana bayous and parishes lined the corridor, and I stopped in front of one photo of a dock where I knew two men lost their lives.

Shudders rippled through my body, trying to shake away the cold memories of a lake in New Orleans from a few months ago. That was the real story anyway. How I managed to off two grown men. And Jaxon. We can't forget about Jaxon.

"Been there before?" Kathleen asked as she slowed next to me and stared at the picture.

"No," I said and kept walking with a snicker.

We turned one more corner and entered a large room filled with computers, dry erase boards, croissants, coffee, and white men.

"Everyone, this is Indigo. But you can call her Indy." Kathleen smiled in my direction.

"Running late, are we?" a slim man asked. It sounded more like a joke than an actual question. His blue eyes danced as he poked at my tardiness.

"I never got the email!" My cheeks flushed red from anger.

"It's cool. I always get here early. I can text you a reminder if you'd like. We should probably exchange numbers anyway, since we're allegedly teammates and everything."

He said *allegedly,* like he, himself couldn't believe we were teammates, He looked me up and down the same way Kathleen did moments ago. His southern accent was thick like grits, but he was all salt—no sugar.

Theodora would call him a car salesman. Whenever someone spoke and we couldn't tell if they were serious or spinning us, she called them a car salesman. I stifled back a giggle. Theodora and I were roommates last year in the Titus University dorms, but she had her own place this year. She was a big time track star these days. Since they won a championship for the school, her prize was bragging rights and her choice of the nicest apartments for on-campus housing. She would have a field day with this guy. Theodora still asked tons of questions about Mr. Chestnut and I didn't have the patience to pretend with her. I just didn't have it in me. Maybe our second year of college would keep her busy enough to forget about her missing track coach.

"Hi Indy, I'm Tristan Rullan. And this is my strange friend, Bryce Fuller," Tristan said, slapping his friend's back. Bryce. The asshole-car salesman was Bryce.

"Alright team! Now that everyone has met, let's make magic!" Harper bellowed.

She flurried from her glass office with her assistant behind her, scribbling things down on an iPad. Not long ago, she was slumming it in the theater's front where she was the secretary, and now she was the supervisor of interns at a mid-sized publishing and newspaper company for Titus University's largest print subsidiary off campus. She was still up to her same antics as she flitted by me in black leather pants, a large belt, and oversized tucked men's shirt. Her love for pins was forever, and she had at least a dozen attached to her shirt, displaying her love for Black Lives Matter and Pro-Choice.

"Indy, I'm so sorry, my love. Since you were added late, your name wasn't on the group email thread. I forgot to tell you the new start time when we had lunch yesterday." Harper slumped her shoulders.

"Lunch yesterday, huh, my old-fashioned nepotism?" Bryce frowned and gave a dry laugh.

I ignored his comment. "It's okay," I nodded, even though my feet curled in my new, ugly work shoes. I crammed my toes inside and stretched the leather from side to side. I instantly regretted buying them. They were not me, but when I went shopping with Theodora and our other friend, Naomi, they

agreed that if you worked in corporate America, you had to have at least one pair of ugly work shoes.

"We don't have to play any of those dumb *'getting to know you' games, right?'"* Bryce asked. He folded his arms and leaned back in his chair, sizing up Harper with the same intensity he'd given me.

"No, Mr. Fuller. I thought I would leave that up to you guys," Harper explained. "You have two options here at Synergy as an intern. You will need to create three non-fiction pieces per semester, with the first assignment due next week. We need something with some meat and potatoes that we can publish in the bi-monthly Titus University Newspaper. Also, leave me your birthdays and birth times so I can make sure we celebrate your special day when the time comes. Otherwise, you kids have fun!" Harper was tossing a ball of rubber bands in the air, while her assistant perspired and feverishly wrote Harper's every word.

"That's it?" Bryce questioned. "How can the first one be due next week and today is the first day?"

"Welcome to the big leagues, Mr. Fuller... was there something else?" Harper looked around.

Tristan cleared his throat. Other teams hustled around us, carrying coffee and stacks of white pages highlighted to hell. "I guess he just means. . . is there like an orientation or something? Do we get computers? Or cubicles?"

"And what time is lunch?" Kathleen added.

"Ahhh, I see, team, I see." Harper winked like she finally understood. "I'm not too sure about that, but I will get back to you. Let me go, uh. Ask someone. Truth be told, it's just my first week here, too." Harper shared a good-natured nudge with Tristan and almost knocked him off the table.

Hours later, when I arrived back at my dorm after my official first day of work, I opened my windows to let the cool air hit my face. I glanced around my room and relief from a long day washed over me. The sun shined directly on my skin, and although the rays felt warm, I tried my best not to be ice. I kicked off my ugly shoes in the closet and grabbed my phone off the nightstand. "Siri, what's Nepotism?" I sounded out as I crashed into my bed.

"Nepotism," Siri, repeated. "It is the practice among those with power or influence of favoring relatives or friends, especially by giving them jobs."

I snorted under my breath.

This was going to be a long day, week, year.

CHAPTER TWO

I LOOKED AT MYSELF in the floor length bathroom mirror at Synergy House. Even though I was wearing tights, they were loose and hung at my bony waist. I always thought I had nice hips and when Chaquille grabbed onto them and held me, I felt like a woman. A woman's woman. The type that a man grabbed and said, *'where do you think you're going?'* I touched my face in the mirror and noticed my sunken, sallow skin. I wasn't eating much these days, and when I slept, I dreamt of Ez. Us fishing, cooking, walking, rowing the boat.

There was a group on campus called the Black Feminist Nation and although they elected me Secretary of our local chapter. I declined the position. It didn't feel complete without Ez being there to watch me become the leader he'd always known me to be. Nothing felt right anymore. With Ez gone, did that mean he was an ancestor? Mama Jackie used to say, *'look to your dreams, that's where you'll find us.'* Heavy pressure tap danced on my chest when I thought about the two of them together—without me.

"Yo, my man. I swear it took up two parking spots," I heard Bryce chuckle when I pulled the heavy bathroom door open and walked toward our office. Tristan was sitting at his desk, clacking away on his keyboard, and his shoulders jumped up and down, snorting at Bryce's comment.

"What are ya'll talking about now?" Kathleen chimed from her computer across from Tristan.

"Did you see that boat in the parking lot? It reminds me of my ex-girl's car. She used to stalk me in this big boat of a vehicle she had. To this day, man, to this day, I power down my cellphone when I'm somewhere working. One time, she showed up to an event I was covering because she tracked my phone. Her old ass car backfired and sent everyone running! I was so embarrassed!" Bryce covered his face with one hand, annoyed at the memory.

"I had to park on the other side of the fence because this humongous bubble took up two spots!" Bryce huffed.

My cheeks reddened. Bryce was talking about The Bus. *My Bus.* An Oldsmobile Cutlass that Ez gave me in high school. It was a gold car with sunspots, and it roared to life from the missing muffler. It was so big I called it The Bus, and a small dent where I had ended a man's life rested right under the bumper, out of sight and out of mind. No one knew that part, though. The Bus was my last tangible connection to Ez. "That's my car, Bryce." I plopped into my chair and shuffled my feet under the desk.

"No, it's not. This thing is huge. It's as long as a boat, I'm telling you." He pointed for us to follow him to the window where he opened his arms in a dramatic fashion.

Kathleen, Tristan, and Bryce peered out of the window when Harper crept behind them. "What's everyone gawking at Indy's car for?" She furrowed her eyebrows.

I didn't look in their direction, but I felt six set of shocked eyes land on me. I gritted my teeth and tried to look busy, while waves of anger washed over me and made my insides

hot. The pressure in my chest was there again. I should really get it checked out at this point.

"Uh, my bad, Indy." Bryce cleared his throat.

"I think that's enough car talk for one day," Harper said with a keen look. Her eyes darted in my direction. I focused on my computer screen and willed myself not to move before I glued my hands around Bryce's neck. I didn't need any voices to feel that; it was all me.

"Has everyone completed their first drafts for the mock print run? I am hoping for something newsworthy." Harper smiled. She wore her hair in two pigtails on either side of her head. She was wearing a jean jumpsuit and a flannel men's shirt tied around her waist. Her famous pins adorned her jeaned outfit. The wrinkles on her face read her age likes rings around a tree trunk, probably from years of smoking too many cigarettes.

"I have mine." Kathleen placed papers on the corner of her desk. Bryce snatched them before Harper could take a peek.

"Let's see what Kathy Girl came up with. Harper only gave us the assignment one week ago, and she's already got all these pages typed and written." Bryce smirked.

"Don't snatch my stuff. And don't call me Kathy Girl." Kathleen glanced around, waiting for Harper to intervene, but she was texting on her phone and paying no attention to the team. She let us come up with pieces to write blind. She didn't ask questions, nor did she assign tasks.

"It helps the creative process. You don't want to lead *too* much. You should let your intuition lead you. Write what you want to write." Harper had clarified. We were on our own, and I weighed what that meant.

"We're all going to read them together anyway, so let's start with yours. . . Ahem." Bryce cleared his throat. "Mental Health and the Haitian Revolution." Bryce read with an exaggerated tone. Before he could continue, Kathleen ripped the paper from his hands; her cheeks were bright red, even through her mocha skin.

"Not cool, man." Tristan shook his head.

"Mr. Fuller, please conduct yourself in a more professional manner. There is no reason for you to patronize another team member. I think it's time for us to do some team-building skills after all." Harper placed her phone face down and frowned at Bryce. Last week, he bragged about going to South Africa with his dad and hunting for lions. A few days after that, I heard him telling Tristan he once dated a black girl and that meant he'd officially had an Oreo sandwich.

Tristan didn't laugh. But he didn't shake his head or look surprised either.

"I was just joking. It's not that serious! You guys have to lighten up if we're supposed to be a team!" Bryce snickered. He looked around incredulously and ran his hands through his hair.

"Mr. Fuller, what is *your* story about?"

He leaned back in his chair and gave a sneaky smile. "That track coach. What was his name? Chestnut? I want to write about that. The school isn't saying what happened, and the news hasn't talked about him in weeks. This man disappeared out of thin air! How Sway? I think we should follow that story!"

"Who is this, Sway?" Harper knitted her brows and her questioning eyes bounced around the room.

Bryce chuckled, while Tristan coughed away a laugh. Kathleen rocked back in her chair, folded her arms, and palmed her crumpled article close to her chest.

As the voices swirled around me, I stopped listening after Bryce said one name. . . *Chestnut.* When I stood in the mirror and stared at myself earlier, parts of me felt bad about what I did to those men. They met their fate from my bare hands.

Fire and water danced in my body; there were so many sides to me that deserved time and attention. Those men weren't worth the air they breathed and the way I saw it—I rid the world of one less issue after another. Why did it have to be up to me to dole out that punishment? I wanted nothing more than to live a typical college life, but I had already collected three bodies. Titus University was still all the buzz after Mr. Chestnut's disappearance. News vans crowded the campus lawn, and the Wellness Center ramped up their *Lunch and Learn* seminars on healthy relationships and intimate partner violence.

I saw his wife, Nurse Meanface, on TV as reporters caught her shuffling from her car with a yoga mat slung over her shoulder and a damp jogger set. She moved back to her childhood home, but it wasn't far enough from Mr. Chestnut's reach. They dissected every part of their marriage but only seemed to blame her in the end, even though she hadn't even accompanied him to the Libra Festival that fateful night. Maybe if she had, things would be different. Maybe *they* wouldn't be different, and she would have been number three. Maybe. They dubbed Mr. Chestnut a handsome coach and family man who got 'caught up' with adoring female athletes. *Who could resist his charm?* Some reporters said. I hated those reports. According to the world—Mrs. Allie Chestnut was mousy and meek. Definitely not a killer, but she couldn't officially be ruled out. No one believed she could kill her husband, and yet hit a yoga class with a swinging ponytail.

Titus released official statements and vowed to help the investigation any way they could. And with all that action, they still had no leads about his whereabouts. I didn't know how to feel about that.

"Indy? Indy? Did you hear me?" Harper frowned.

Once I came to, she was staring at me with curious eyes. "We're going to lead with your story next month. What is yours about? Oh, it doesn't even matter. I know it will be great. That's why you're here."

I cringed a little inside at being caught not paying attention. I needed to be more present before this nepotism thing really gained some legs. Besides, struggling to untangle myself from Chaquille in the morning and the occasional eye roll at Bryce, my first week on the job went well.

"Why are we leading with her story? Shouldn't we vote on something like that?" Bryce scratched his head.

"Yes, that would be fair," I mumbled. Leading with my article? Not a chance. The best I came up with were poems I penned about Ez. They were good poems, but nothing else in my life was newsworthy at the moment. I thought about high-lighting Theodora's championship win, but with Mr. Chestnut being the one who brought the team to their winning glory; his absence would certainly overshadow the actual crowning achievement.

"Are you sure, Indy?" Harper asked with wide eyes.

My face softened, and I dropped my shoulders. When I started my work-study job last year, it was Harper who helped me keep a job when the other supervisors wanted to fire me for being late. Now it was Harper who made sure my writing was seen. She was a good work mom.

And I knew good moms from the bad ones.

A short, chubby Hispanic man walked by my cubicle and the wind that followed him almost knocked me out of my seat. He smelled like pine trees and an earthy, musty scent which smelled like rain sitting on the wooden canoes out front of Ez's house. When it rained, he would laugh and say, *'the veil is thin today, Indy-Lindy.'*

My God, this man never, ever, left my thoughts. I even smelled him.

I stared at my computer and strained my pupils until they twitched. I dared—no, I willed the tears not to fall, but they did. When Harper saw the look on my face, she *knew* without knowing.

"Then we'll lead with Bryce's article. And let's take lunch, team." She clapped her hands together.

"But it's like, 10 a.m.?" Tristan squinted at the clock.

Harper giggled. "I'm a brunch girl myself. Anyone want to order in?"

"I really think we should start nailing down these articles," Bryce pushed. "We only have a few weeks before they are officially due, like you said."

Kathleen said nothing.

I tasted salty tears in the corner of my mouth and I hoped the wetness dried quickly on my face without the rest of the team noticing. I started to dart to the restroom before they could see, but I forgot to sign out of my computer and began fumbling with the mouse. Synergy House had a weird rule that if employees were away from their desk for over five minutes, they were required to sign out of the network and computer entirely. Something about creative integrity, they called it.

"No, let's break for lunch, team. We'll resume after twelve." I heard Harper say as I walked away.

"Two hours?" Bryce hissed and shuffled out of the room.

After lunch, or brunch—I pressed CONFIRM on my phone, from my text message alert, reminding me about my appointment with Trenita. It would be my last session with her for a while. She was having surgery and would be out on leave. When Ez passed away, I think I spent my first three sessions with Trenita totally silent. Like. No words. I nodded here and there as light tears floated down my cheeks. She never pressed,

and she sat there in silence with me. You don't know what it's like to have someone pull you up from the ground and lift your face until you see the light.

Grateful was an understatement.

After I picked up Chaquille from his physical therapy appointment that afternoon, we stripped our clothes down and suspended ourselves in a steam filled shower. He wrung his loofah sponge on my neck, letting suds cascade down my warmed skin. I dropped my head under his touch, and I rested my face in the crook of his neck. My hands instinctively visited the back of his head as I cradled it. Trenita was always saying that I had to be intentional about finding things to be joyful about. I was joyful for Chaquille and honored to be with him. Some days, he was the only thing I felt I could be joyful about. Was that bad? That sometimes he was the only thing that brought me joy since Ez died?

I don't know.

After our shower, I lay in bed, while Chaquille snored beside me. My thoughts turned to thinking about my girls, Theodora and Naomi, a few blocks over. Naomi and her girlfriend, Ivelisse, got their own spot off campus. When I returned to school weeks into the Fall semester, I had to go before the school's advisory board and petition for full-time student status, and special permission to live on campus again. They weren't too fond of me abandoning my dorm room and all my things, but when Ez died, I wasn't sure where I wanted to be. So, I stayed in Tunica Rivers. I lucked out when a new transfer backed out of housing, and I got my own dorm room, and it was co-ed.

My phone buzzed, and I reached over Chaquille's snoring body and grabbed it.

> **DAD:** Try to be home early tomorrow.
> We'll have visitors.

I started to text my dad back, but I clicked my phone off and laid down next to Chaquille. I snuggled up close to him. Since Mom broke out of Trochesse, Home for the Criminally Insane Asylum, and Ez's death, people were always visiting the house for one reason or another. I didn't have the energy for it. I inhaled Chaquille's after-shower smell and closed my eyes, drifting off to sleep. I hoped Ez would be there.

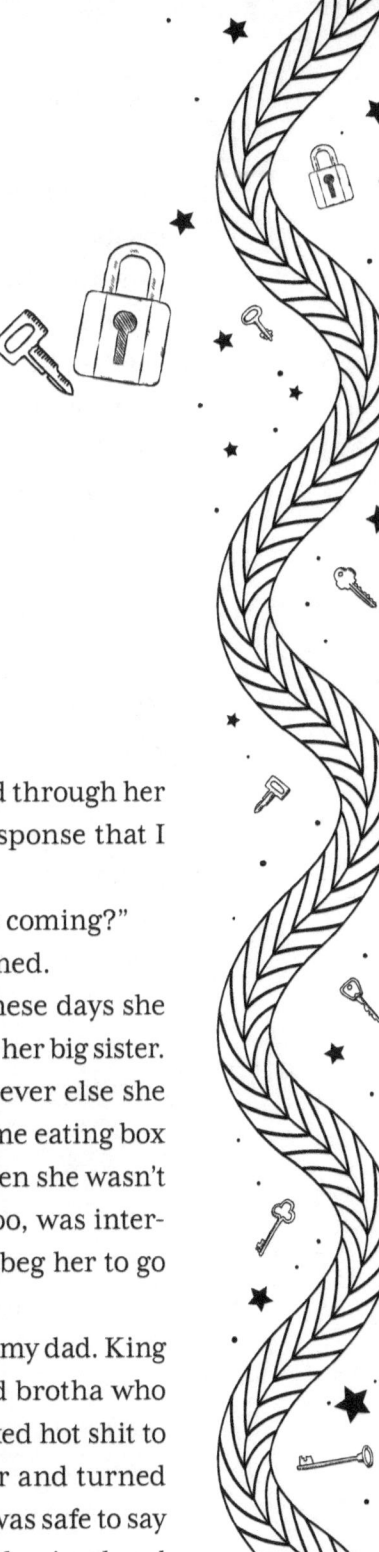

CHAPTER THREE

"**A**RE YOU READY?" I asked Sidney.

My thirteen-year-old sister scrolled through her phone and grunted an inaudible response that I took to mean yes.

"Should I pick you up on Sunday or is Prince coming?"

"I'll have Prince take me home." Sidney yawned.

My little athlete was getting chubby, and these days she preferred her half-brothers; Prince and Trent to her big sister.

She played field hockey, softball, and whatever else she could—but these days after Ez. . . she stayed home eating box mac and cheese and playing on her phone. When she wasn't home, she lounged at her dad's house. That, too, was interesting because we used to have to damn near beg her to go see him any other day.

I was dropping her off before heading to help my dad. King was Sidney's dad. He was a tall, light-skinned brotha who licked his lips too much. You could tell he ranked hot shit to himself. When Sidney and I loaded up the car and turned down his long, manicured driveway, I guess it was safe to say he was well off. King and Mom used to sing together in a band

called The FatCats. She toured all over the south, performing in clubs and bars. She was in a relationship with Dad during this time, but she popped up pregnant anyway and along came Sidney. When Sidney decided to live with us instead of her dad, King, didn't object. I guess with two older sons, who were also in the family business and musically inclined; he didn't have space for a sporty daughter.

Dad spent long days huffing and puffing, building her a bedroom in our already too small house. I looked out of the window, half expecting Mom to come barreling out of King's house. We still didn't know where she was and I'm sure that's what Dad wanted to talk about today after I dropped off Sidney. My chest burned, and I gagged it away when I thought about where my mom could be.

We spent weekends as a family waiting for Ms. Arletha to pop. The doctor's got her due date wrong and we were still anxiously awaiting the arrival of a new face. I wanted to make sure I was home for the big event. Ms. Arletha and Dad opted to wait to find out the gender of their first child together until the baby was born. I had never heard of such a thing, but they wanted to be surprised. Between Ez's death, Mom on the run, and worrying about us; Ms. Arletha's pregnancy had not been easy. Since Ez passed away and the pain in my chest started, Tunica Rivers felt like it was closing in on me, and everywhere I went I found traces of him.

I threw The Bus into park in front of King's house. I patted the dashboard and smiled. It held just as many secrets as it did miles. Ironically, it was then that I thought of Ez the most; when I was driving. His scent permeating through the seats and he always said, *'these old beaters can take a hit. It's those new cars that ain't worth two nickels.'* He was right. The Bus could take a hit. And it did. Oh, it did.

"Hi Trent," I said, pulling Sidney's bag from the car and

handing them to him. Sidney hopped out of the passenger side and strolled into the house without a glance behind her.

"Uh, bye Sidney." I squinted.

"Oh, my bad. Bye Indy-Lindy." Sidney hustled back to the car offering a weak kiss on the cheek.

"What's up with her?" Trent asked. He was a younger version of his dad in every way. Tall, smooth, and a light bright.

"I'm not sure." I shook my head. "She said your dad is taking her home on Sunday?" I confirmed.

"Yeah, or Prince will. You know, he just got his license."

"Okay, see you then." I waved.

I popped in the address my dad gave me and I met him grinning outside of a dilapidated house.

"So, what do you think?" he asked with wide eyes. His excitement brimmed as he shifted from one foot to the other and waited for my response. The house was small and old. It was a weird shade of pale blue, and it was missing quite a few shingles and screens in the windows.

"It's okay, I guess," I said, pensively.

"It doesn't look like much, but with the insurance money that Ez left, it was enough to buy this house and one more around your school. Me and 'Letha figured it was time for us to stop slaving for other people. We're going to be landlords. Get us some tenants and rent these babies out." Dad grinned.

"A landlord?" my eyes were wide. My dad knew nothing about being a landlord and I was sure he would somehow drag me into this.

"Yeah. it could be a family business. You know I can fix things that need fixin' and with you, Sidney, and Arletha putting your women's touch on things and making it pretty,

I figured we could make this little house into something presentable and rent it out to a nice family. Besides, I think it would be good. For all of us. We need something to take our minds off. . . off Ez."

I looked up at the house and sighed. It needed a lot of work. More than a lot of work. It would need a lot of money. I spied the broken paint spatter and markings on the cement where there had clearly been water damage. I also checked out my dad, beaming from ear to ear. He needed this, and I guess he thought we all did. Dad had worked at the Tunica Rivers Retirement Home almost all of my life. He worked until his hands were black, and dirt collected under his nails. No matter how much he washed his hands, it was like dirt permeated through his pores. He said it proved he was a hardworking man, but now, decades later, he walked with a hunch from years of lifting, bending, and fixing things. When Ez was killed, it was a blip on the tv stations. Mr. Chestnut's disappearance was still big news even months later, but when the police killed my grandfather, I saw one news station cover the story, and they referred to him as a developmentally delayed man with ongoing mental health issues. Trochesse Police Department offered a settlement that made me vomit. There was no amount of money that would bring him back, and I abhorred my dad for even accepting the puny number. Dad was a decent handyman and could slap up some walls as needed, but an entire house? Landlords? I didn't have the heart to tell him my real thoughts.

"Okay, Dad, what do you need?"

"My girl!" He clapped his hands. "I made a list of things we need from the hardware store. When Sidney gets back from her dad's she can help too, and of course Arletha can't do much, but once the baby is born, she can come and help paint or something. I have a few work buddies who said they would stop by too. We need all hands-on deck for this project, and then we'll start the second property." Dad was rambling a mile a minute and I could tell he had been watching lots of HGTV.

For the next three hours, I moved furniture, swept floors, ripped up carpets, and sweated out my hair. I cut it down short to my nape, and I kept putting my hands to my neck since I was used to feeling the weight of my braids. There were no more braids holding me down, and hopefully nothing else would. Once we finished, I followed Dad back to Ez's house, which still had police tape around it. I held my breath as we entered the home and my eyes stung from the tears I knew would fall. Dad had the keys in his hand.

"Indy, Ez left you the house. It was in his will. I didn't even know he had one," Dad chuckled. He handed me the house keys, but I didn't reach for them. They gleaned in Dad's hands and I felt like if I touched them, the feelings of that night would come rushing back to me like a ton of bricks that never really went away. Neither did the heavy pressure in my chest that I swallowed down.

"Indy. . . are you still seeing the counselor at school? It would be good for you to talk to someone."

I took the keys from Dad and shoved them deep where they burned in my pocket. I told my dad I started seeing Trenita after Ez died, but not about the sessions before. "I'm okay, Dad. I'm fine." I held my breath and nodded.

"Are you sure? Should I call one of those deans and ask to get you some help?"

"What kind of help?" I bit the inside of my cheek.

"Well, you started the semester late. Because of Ez and all. I know you probably have to make up a lot of work. Thank God for that paid internship. That takes a load off. But are you okay, Indy?"

"I'm okay, Dad, really."

No, she ain't, Ben! a voice in me whispered. I swallowed it away. Whenever I heard the voices, I tried to really stop and listen. With Mom still missing, I took every voice seriously.

There were two boxes sitting on the front step labeled *'for Indy-Lindy.'* Not wanting to see what was inside, I crept to it. It was probably something that would make me need to throw up. When I peeked into the box, a picture of Ez, Mama Jackie, and I sat on top. I picked it up and a tear fell onto the picture. I remembered the day clearly. Mama Jackie and Ez took me to a fair, and I was eating cotton candy with it sticking out the sides of my mouth. My smile was big and my mouth was red from water ice. Ez was scowling. No older than ten, I remember offering him some and he said, *'Men don't eat cotton candy, and I'm a man, girl!'* He smiled and his missing teeth made me giggle the rest of the night. I was happy. We were happy.

"And. . . there is an investigator coming. I told him we would be here working. He wants to talk about your mom," Dad interrupted.

"What about her? Have they found her?"

"No, they haven't. Yet. A few days ago, they came by the house to interview us. They thought we were helping her hide. Even though it's Trochesse's policy to notify the public about a missing mental health patient, they're not going to right now."

"Why?"

Dad sighed. "Well, that lady nurse and her missing husband, for one. And now your mom is on the run. They already had complaints and lawsuits filed for inhumane treatment of the patients. The state thought things were already too hot, and this story would just take public opinion over the edge. Trochesse hired a private investigator to search for her instead."

Mr. Chestnut strikes again.

They weren't doing a formal search for Mom because Mr. Chestnut's disappearance already made the state look bad. He was married to the head of nursing at Trochesse after all. Allie Chestnut was Nurse Meanface. At least to me she was. His disappearance outshined my mom's. I took in my dad's words as another car pulled up outside and slammed the door. A heavyset, white man with too many gold chains around his neck walked onto Ez's-now-turned-our property. He pushed past the police tape and the freshly coated paint on the walls peeled off a little with the tape. Right where Ez's body laid months prior.

I winced.

"I see your dad has explained to you why I'm here." The man smiled. "My name is Minko Forrest. Trochesse: Home for the Criminally Insane hired me to help find your mom, Ms. Lewis. Do you have any idea where she could be? I've been able to hold them off, but they want her found as soon as possible since, you know. She poses a threat to society. I don't want to see her harmed. Your dad tells me you and her are close and she often writes letters?"

Minko looked me in my eyes straight away. He didn't linger on my face or glance around to check out my body. He was here to do his job, and I liked him immediately. Too bad he needed help to take down Mom because I was not the girl for the job. I wouldn't help him capture my mom. Besides, I didn't have any information. Mom hadn't written me a letter in months since before they killed Ez. I scratched my head and shifted under the hot Louisiana sun. Paint splatter rested on my forehead, and I wiped it with the back of my hand. He showed up hours after we started painting, and I smelled and sweated like I was being interrogated about the murders of three men.

They had it coming

"I really don't know where she is. She hasn't reached out to me in months. What do you think they'll do if they find her?" A headache instantly formed. So many things could go wrong with this scenario.

"Well, they'll return her to Trochesse and maybe even move her to a different facility, you know, since she knows how to bust out and all. You have my word, Ms. Lewis and Mr. Barre. Here is my card. If you have any information or hear from her, please give a ring. I will do my best to make sure she's not hurt."

Minko extended a card in Dad's direction. Once he drove off, Dad and I shared a long glance. Mom was giving Trochesse a run for their money when she was and *wasn't* there. She made them look incompetent by breaking out of a locked down facility. If the situation were different or anyone else's mother, I would probably find it funny. But it was my mom, and it wasn't funny.

Dad's phone rang and broke our gaze.

"Hello?" he said. I heard voices on the other end and Dad's tone became faster. "Okay, we'll be there soon! I'm knee deep in paint, but we'll be there!" he shouted.

"What happened?"

"'Letha is having the baby! Let's get to the hospital! You're about to be a big, big sister, Indy-Lindy!"

CHAPTER FOUR

WHEN I LOOKED into her small, brown eyes, my heart burst. Paisley Sage Barre was born in the same hospital as me and Sidney. A girl. Ms. Arletha and Dad had a girl.

"Look at her pink cheeks! Can I hold her?" Sidney beamed. It was the first time I had seen her smile in weeks.

Ms. Arletha was in the hospital bed with a tired but glowing face. They wrapped Paisley in a small, yellow blanket like a burrito and she carefully lifted Paisley and handed her to Sidney.

"Hi Paisley, I'm your big sister, Sidney." Sidney rocked in place with Paisley in her arms. "I can show you how to play softball and field hockey when you get older. And your big, big sister, Indy-Lindy, can show you how to be a writer. And she's good at everything. And Ez. . ."

"Ez is here too. He is always around us." Ms. Arletha nodded with tears in her eyes. "Hand me that tissue box over there, honeydew."

Dad was staring at Paisley with a new intensity that I hadn't seen in a while. "Sit down, Sidney. Don't want you tripping with Ms. Paisley. I want to talk to my ladies—all of them."

Sitting down in a chair across the room, I studied my dad to see what he was up to now. His eyes were deep-set brown with circular laugh lines around his mouth. He was getting older. We all were.

Dad cleared his throat. "Our family has been through so much these past few years. With your mom being gone and Ez being murdered, it's been a lot for our family. One thing God has blessed us with is 'Letha. She has changed our home, and now given us the most precious gift yet, our Paisley."

As if she knew her name already, Paisley cooed in Sidney's arms, making Sidney giggle and smile wide. I snapped a picture and texted it to Theodora and Naomi.

"I've been thinking. We shouldn't keep working for other people. I spent my entire life building and fixing things for others, and now with the insurance money that Ez left, I believe it's officially time for me to step out onto my own, and make sure that we have something to leave our family. Indy and 'Letha already know, but I purchased two homes, and Ez left Indy his house in the will. The plan is to fix them up and rent 'em out. I've never been no landlord or done nothing like this. I had my buddy from the retirement home run the numbers. He is into stuff like that. Could've been an accountant or something but just like me, he wasted years of his life at the retirement home doing something he didn't love. This will be our family business, and something that is our own. It belongs to us. I'll need my girls' help. But together, we can do it." Dad's smile was sheepish and red.

Ms. Arletha inhaled, and before long, a fat tear stained her tired face. "Together. We'll all do it together," she said through her happy tears.

Paisley cooed again, and Dad and I crowded around Sidney as she rocked back and forth in the chair beside Ms. Arletha's bed.

A new face in the family. A new little person to love, to teach. To protect. How did you keep a girl safe? Boys were a little easier to manage. They didn't have to worry about the same things that girls did. "Do you want to hold her, Indy?" Sidney asked.

Shifting my weight, I held out my arms. "Of course!"

Sidney stood and carefully handed Paisley to me. Staring into her wide and wondrous eyes, I'd have no issues protecting her. I was Indy-Lindy; the big, big sister. She would be protected from bullies like Bryce, predators like Mr. Chestnut, and fuck-boys like Jaxon. We would all work together and make sure Paisley was healthy, happy, and loved. We would watch her grow. Help her grow. Ez and Mama Jackie included from the other side. "Hi Ms. Paisley. We are so happy to meet you."

Paisley yawned widely and her pink tongue hung out of her mouth.

We all laughed.

I studied all her little features and hands, and toes. She was beautiful. Just beautiful. I handed Paisley back to Ms. Arletha as she and Dad ohh and ahhed in her delicate face.

I stepped into the long corridor as nurses mulled around me. There was a small waiting area at the end of the hallway, so I walked toward it with tears blurring my sight. There was another one of us here, and Ez couldn't see it. I pulled out my phone and dialed one number. I had memorized it for years by heart. He knew me better than I knew myself, and even if he wasn't talking to me—I still wanted him to know.

The phone rang four times before his voicemail picked up. This was the fourth message I left him in a few months. He was in his second year of a lengthy apprenticeship to be a plumber. At least he was the last time we spoke. He came to Ez's funeral with his parents and paid his condolences, but otherwise we had no conversation. When I chose Chaquille

over Will last year, I had made a choice. I wanted to explore things with Chaquille and see where our relationship took us. I didn't know it would mean the end of my best friendship with Will.

"Hey Will. . . it's me. . . Indy, again. I just wanted to tell you. Ms. Arletha had the baby. It's a girl, and she named her Paisley. She's so beautiful, Will. She has my dad's face and little chubby cheeks. . . Anyway. I just wanted to let you know. . . I hope you're okay. Call me if you want to talk. I miss you."

I pressed end and walked back to Ms. Arletha's room.

CHAPTER FIVE

WHEN CHAQUILLE BARRELED out of the large double doors, a goofy smile spread across his face. Picking him up from physical therapy weekly interrupted my work schedule, but it was okay with me. He swung the door open and hopped inside, sinking the weight of The Bus.

"Hey babe! They said I'm getting better at the leg presses. I even went up a few weights. You know, you should really think about coming along for a session or two. Those birds in there be throwing it at me. And I always say, 'no—not me. I'm with my one and only girl, Indigo Lewis. Writer Extraordinaire, done cut off all her hair!'"

I threw my head back and showed all my teeth. Slapping Chaquille's arm, I said, "Who is throwing it at you? Boy, don't make me come in there! I've ended people for less!" I joked. But damn. . . if he *only* knew.

"Oh, you've ended people for less, huh?! Well, how about you end those flapping gums and start the car so we can roll. I'm hungry." He smirked.

Ever since Chaquille's seizure, the school let him take a reduced schedule with online classes. We hoped he would be back to almost normal after one month, but one turned into two and he was still at it with weekly sessions. "I just want to get back to DJ'ing, man." Chaquille rapped on the dashboard and moved his mouth in and out of circles, making beats.

"And what about your classes?" I put on my blinker and looked in the rearview mirror so I could make a u-turn.

"Those too, woman. I have to get back to those, too. But for right now, I'm on stage with DJ Khaled and we're doing his dance together. The energy is good. The crowd is going wild. And you're standing off to the side trying to dance. That's how it's going down!" He beat on the dashboard and used a pencil to tap on the window.

Chaquille's vision for himself made me giggle again as I pressed harder on the gas, heading toward Titus University. He had it all figured out for himself, despite any pesky medical conditions like epilepsy holding him back. The night it all happened still brought a chill down to my toes. I looked over at Chaquille as I took our exit to get on the highway. To think that I could've lost him too, the same night that I lost Ez was a thought that made me shudder.

"Are you sure you don't want to come?" I was heading back to Tunica Rivers for the night after I dropped him off because I wanted to spend more time with Paisley. She was so freaking cute. I checked the time on my phone. Theodora was coming with me to Tunica Rivers, and I had to pick her up soon.

"No, you spend time with your little sister. I'll be good." He smiled. He leaned in and kissed me on the forehead. "You be careful going home, okay?"

I smiled and kissed him back.

Later that day, I was holding Paisley and feeding her a bottle. Her doe, brown eyes searched my face and her tiny finger wrapped around mine, holding on for dear life. I loved this little face. By the looks of my old bedroom, turned into Sidney and Paisley's new bedroom, the family had made room for Paisley in the house and in their hearts. My old room was the master bedroom of the house, but when Sidney moved in from King's house, Dad was ever the handyman and converted the large closet into a tiny bedroom for Sidney. Now that I was living at Titus and only visiting, they had converted the room even further and now Paisley's crib, bassinet, and dressers took up most of the room while Sidney opted to keep her closet.

"What a beauty," Theodora said, making kissy faces at Paisley over my shoulder.

"Isn't she, though?" This kid had an army behind her and she didn't even know it yet.

"Your boy came to our team meeting the other day."

"My boy who?" I rolled my eyes and neck hard, feeling like she was about to say some bullshit.

"Bryce. Uhh. Fuller is it?"

The car salesman.

"What did he want?" I snorted and rose from the rocking chair to switch spots with Theodora. How did she know him? She plopped down in the chair and adjusted the pillows behind her back while I place Paisley gently in her arms. She's sound asleep.

"He said he's writing an article about Mr. Chestnut. Something about the police not doing a thorough enough investigation. He wanted to interview members of the track team."

"Oh?" My interest piqued. Bryce was really giving this thing with Mr. Chestnut steam.

"I feel bad. I mean, I know all the things they say about him in the newspaper, but he was so nice to me and the girls on

the team. What if something *did* happen, Indy? We were all so close to him. What if it was one of the girls, or a deranged fan? Like Selena or something?"

I snorted again. "Please never compare Mr. Chestnut to the Queen Selena." Was Theodora serious right now? I *told* her he was a teacher at my high school, and I *told* her he had a history of sexing the young girls and not getting caught. I had told her damn near everything except that I clocked him upside the head, filled his coat with fish, and sent him to meet his maker late one night in New Orleans. She still believed him to be the victim here?

"I'm just saying it's plausible." She shrugged and raised her eyebrows.

"Theodora, you always had a soft spot for him. The facts are he was a predator, plain and simple. Whatever happened to him was probably karma."

I paced in front of my window before I heard a car door close. When I peered outside, I saw King make his way to the front step. He was alone. The hairs on the back of my neck stood up as I studied him through the curtains, wondering why he was here. He rarely made it to our side of the town where the much smaller houses were, and he only came to drop off Sidney. And he definitely never got out of the car and walked up to our house. He was a taller version of Sidney and they all shared the same light-skinned, freckled features. King looked so different from my short, pudgy, brown-skinned dad. Mom didn't have a type, clearly. If you loved her, she loved you; and that was that.

He knocked on the door, and I heard Ms. Arletha greet him. "Hello Mr. King."

"Hi King, Sidney is at school for field-hockey," my dad said. He came from the shed outside in knee-length rubber boots, an old construction belt, and a shirt that said *The FatCats*.

King looked him up and down before responding. "Hey Ben. Yeah, I know Sid is in school. Can we talk? You and I?"

Dad studied King for a second before he wiped his dirty hands on a dish towel. Ms. Arletha grimaced as he placed the dirty towel on her pristine counter. Dad nodded and motioned with his head for King to follow him. Ms. Arletha and I stole worried glances at each other and lovey dovey faces at Paisley.

After a few minutes, Dad's voice got louder, and quick steps pounded across the floor. The back door swung open, and King came storming through.

"Ladies!" He nodded without looking in our direction. Dad stormed back into the room; his eyes red with fury.

"What happened?"

"And what are you wearing?" Ms. Arletha asked, peering at his toolbelt and boots.

"King wants to take Sidney back. He wants her to live with him and he's going to get custody of her!" Dad paced the hallway.

My stomach churned, and I had to lean on the wall for support. "What? Why?" I managed.

"He said it's not safe here. Because of your mom being on the loose. . . because of Ez being killed."

"But I thought you said that he dropped her off one day after he decided he wanted to go on tour? I thought he said he didn't want to raise a daughter? That's how Sidney came to live here to begin with, right?" Ms. Arletha shot questions between me and Dad. She was trying to make sense of it, but there was none that I could see.

"That is what he said!" The anger in my tone was hot and ready to fight.

"He's changed his mind. He said her brothers are older and they are going to help take care of her. She'll have better opportunities with him, and he'll be able to keep an eye on her."

"This is bullshit!" I screamed. I wanted my family intact, and it included Sidney in the count. The day was stuck in my brain, rent free. When Sidney was born, she lived with King and Mom. When Mom would go off on her disappearing acts, King decided he couldn't take care of baby Sidney. Her older brothers, Prince and Trent, were musicians too. Trent played the drums and Prince could dance and play the piano. They were a low budget *Jackson 5*, only Sidney didn't have a musical bone in her body. She was an athlete through and through. When it became too much for King to manage, while trying to chase down Mom, he asked Dad to take in Sidney and raise her with me, her big sister. That was about five years ago. Mom had been locked away in Trochesse for almost the same amount of time. It wasn't easy or even fun giving up my room, but Sidney and I were close, and we made it work. Or so I thought. *Wait, does she want to live with her dad?* Had she told him that?

"Dad? What does Sidney want?"

He hung his head between his shoulders and paused. "King said he talked it over with her and she wants to live with him."

"My lands!" Ms. Arletha gasped.

The air escaped my chest as I dejectedly sat in the chair and rocked Paisley. Sidney wanted to leave us. *Us?*

CHAPTER SIX

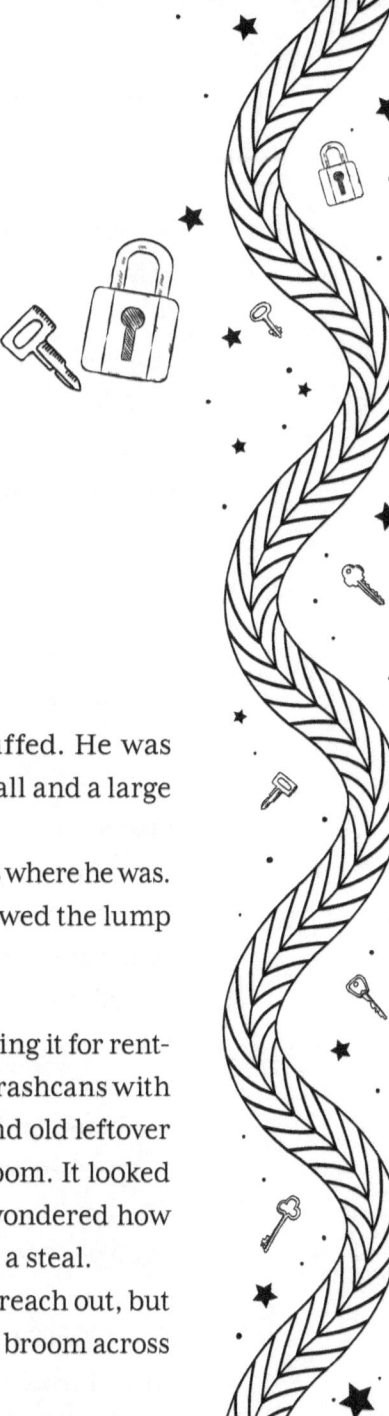

"**H**OW'S THAT WILL doing?" Dad huffed. He was plunging a hammer into the back wall and a large hole formed.

Will was never too far from my thoughts. That's where he was.

"Still not talking to me," I admitted. I swallowed the lump in my throat.

"You know you hurt that boy, Indy."

Dad and I were working on the house preparing it for renters. We filled the tiny space with debris, large trashcans with all kinds of wood pieces stuck out of the top, and old leftover furniture, and half-ripped carpet dated the room. It looked like no one had been inside for years, and I wondered how much dad spent on this house; it was probably a steal.

"I know, I hurt him, Dad. I've been trying to reach out, but he doesn't want to hear from me." I scraped the broom across the floor harder.

"Well, make it right, Indy. That boy has always loved you. I know you like this Chaquille fella, and he's nice and all, even with the epilepsy thing, but don't forget the people who have always been around."

"I know Dad, I know." I was glad Theodora stayed home with Ms. Arletha and Paisley. She had been on my ass too about the way things ended with Will. No one felt more guilty than me. But how could I get him to talk to me when he wouldn't even respond to my calls or texts?

"After everything with Ez. . . we have to make sure we tell people we care for how we feel about them. We have to take care of each-other." He swatted at the small hole even harder and grunted as his short arms connected with the wall. "I care about you, Indy. I love you. But you have to open up."

I gripped the broom and choked away fire in my throat. *Was it heartburn that I had?*

Behind Dad's head, I noticed a chain and what looked like a small closet. "What is that?" I pointed.

Dad swung around and examined the crawl space he had just blasted into with his hammer. "What is that?" He poked his head into the small opening. "Ahhh! It's a dumbwaiter."

"A dumbwaiter? Who is a dumbwaiter? That sounds like something Ez would say. . ." I chuckled.

Dad gave a forced smile, his just as heavy as mine. "A dumb-waiter is an old-school pulley system. For maids. They used it back in the old days to pull food trays or laundry up through the house and out of the way of prying eyes."

I peeked my head into the hole and looked up and down. The chains attaching the flat wooden slats looked rickety from years of nonuse. Something had chewed through the wood and there were splinters on the edges. "I thought they used these things for mansions and stuff? This house is tiny." I frowned.

"Don't be talking about our generational wealth like that, girl!" Dad chuckled. "We're going to get this house into tip-top shape for renters! You never know, they might like something like this!" Dad hopped in place from the excitement.

"If you say so." I pulled my head from the hole and surveyed the room. "We still have a lot to do."

"You're right. I been watching YouTube videos to put in this garbage disposal. They had a construction class downtown, but I've been keeping Tunica Rivers Retirement Home standing all these years as their handyman. Surely I can figure this place out for myself." Dad looked around the room and all the mess.

"Ez would love a project like this," I muttered.

Dad nodded and slammed the hammer into a new section of the wall, forgetting about the dumbwaiter. "He would. He would."

The next day, I twiddled my thumbs at Synergy House. Harper was so frazzled after Tristan used the word, *there*, incorrectly in an article, that she called an entire team meeting and forced me and Theodora back from Tunica Rivers early.

I yawned as I looked out the window and rain littered the glass. Who called an afternoon meeting at 5pm? *My Harper.*

"Now team, going forward, let's make sure we remember, *there* is a place, and *their* is ownership. Okay?"

"Okay," we said in unison. Tristan's face was especially pale.

"Harper, did you get a chance to edit my article? I think you'll find minimal mistakes from me." Bryce shrugged.

Tristan dropped his shoulders, and Bryce slapped his neck with a snort.

"I had to dig in, my man." Bryce chuckled.

Tristan sat stone-faced.

"I've read no articles yet, at least fully. I perused Tristan's, that's it. I have been consumed with grief about what is going on in our world with Black Lives Matter and the abortion bans. What is the world coming to? It's just all too much." Harper

shook her head, and her large, pink earrings jiggled. Today she wore lime green tights with a matching swisher windbreaker. She wrapped a pink headband around her head and her hair was in a ponytail to one side. She would look like a jazzed-up gym teacher if it wasn't for her everlasting love for pins stuck to her jacket.

"Harper, so you haven't read our articles because you are sad about the news?" Bryce scrunched his face, and his freckles moved around.

I hated how he said her name. Harper O'Sullivan insisted we call her by her first name when the other teams called their supervisors by Miss or Mister. Harper said, *'I'm a cool boss. We don't need those stuffy titles,'* and scoffed at the thought. When Bryce said her name, it didn't sound cool. It sounded like disrespect. Maybe I was thinking too much into things, but as I glanced over at Kathleen watching the exchange between Harper and Bryce, I knew she saw it, too.

"Mr. Fuller, please take the creative process into consideration when you are attempting to be productive. I cannot produce content if I am stressed. I would also encourage *you* to only create when you feel your best. Thank you for your concern. Indy, please stick around. I would like to discuss something with you. Meeting is adjourned." Harper waved her hands.

"Is she serious right now?" Bryce sucked his teeth.

"Come on, Bryce." Kathleen sighed and motioned to the door.

Tristan was stuffing things into his bag and avoiding eye contact with Bryce as they walked out.

When I gathered my things and made my way to Harper's glassed-in office, I plopped into her leather chair as she shut the door behind us.

"What was that about?" I quizzed.

"Who? Bryce? I'm not worried about that young man. He has to learn respect. He doesn't hurt me." Harper cheesed and gave an exaggerated smile.

"I love what you've done with the place," I said. They gave Harper a large corner office, and the people walking outside below looked like ants with us being on the tenth floor.

Harper stood. "Do you see all of this, Indy? I get to look out into the world! Not stuck in some stuffy windowless office like back at the theater." She placed her hand on the large windows and peered outside. "After spending years in the Titus theater, this is such a treat. I'm going to bring my energy to this place. We need to liven it up a little. That's what I wanted to talk to you about."

I shifted in my seat, unsure of what she had in mind. "Meaning?"

"How are you? Since Ez?" She leaned in close and placed her folded hands under her chin.

Needles shot to my head, and I felt blinding whiteness. I rubbed my temples and rocked in my chair. I felt a headache coming on. My lips pursed into a tight line and I focused my eyes behind Harper at another skyscraper from her window. How did you tell someone that you still had dreams of mermaids, and Grandpa Ez? You bite your nails at the thought of your sister leaving you next? How did I tell anyone, anything? If hanging on was a person, I would be the mascot.

"I'm. . . okay. I guess. Managing." I gritted my teeth and lied through my pain.

"Are you sure? Let me know if this is ever too much for you. I wanted to see if you were interested in writing a special interest piece. Something about the grief process."

"Grief?" I gave a quizzical look. Trenita said the word frequently and as much as I loved words, that was one I wasn't

sure described me. I always smiled and nodded, but never really understood what it meant.

"You know; grief. After you lose someone, you feel anger. Sadness. Sorrow," Harper said—each word softer than the next, and I knew she was trying to spare my feelings. They felt like daggers, anyway.

When I said nothing, Harper continued. "Mental Health Week is coming up, and I thought you could use your pain as your message and write about your experience and how you've been able to carry on after such a loss." Harper sipped her large coffee as she waited with bated breath for my reaction.

Carry on? Was I carrying on? Instinctually, I placed my hand to my head to twirl a braid, but I forgot I had chopped off all my hair. Now sulking, my hand fell back into my lap and picked at a hangnail. "I don't know. I guess I can come up with something. How much time do I have?"

"How about one month?"

I nodded. "I can try." And I would try. For Harper, I would try.

I walked back to The Bus—taking up two parking spots—and I plopped into the seat. I took out my phone, and I searched for *grief*. It read:

> deep sorrow, especially that
> caused by someone's death.

Grief. So that's what this feeling in my chest was called. I was grieving.

CHAPTER SEVEN

FALL SEMESTER BUSTLED by, but some things remained the same.

'I know'd you ain't still sleeping in that lair, girl. Do you need some Moon juice? Talk to the stars, girl.' Ez bellowed in my dream. I twisted my legs in the blankets as his voice stirred me awake. I palmed my neck, now damp with sweat and grabbed for a water bottle sitting next to my bed. It contorted as I gulped and took large swigs.

Another dream about Ez.

I glanced over at Chaquille, lightly snoring. The sun was making its way through the blinds. I reached out and caressed his face, where the sun was already touching him. We went to sleep early last night. I was trying to keep a better schedule, so I didn't feel rushed in the morning and that included an earlier bedtime. This was of course, with the help and careful planning of Trenita. After I told her I wasn't taking the medication anymore she said we had to come up with goals to help me create quieter moments in my day. Some of the stuff she said was fluff and all therapy-like. If the alternative took medication, which made me sleep through life—I would try it.

My phone buzzed, and when I grabbed it and swiped up, little Miss Paisley lit up my screen. Dad was holding her and he was half asleep and deliriously happy from too many days spent renovating houses by way of YouTube. I smiled at his smile.

"What are you over there smiling about into your phone first thing in the morning?" Chaquille leaned over my shoulder.

I pushed him away. "Bye! That breath is still asleep?" I scrunched my face.

Chaquille blew his breath in my face while I squirmed to get away. "Are we meeting today for lunch?" he breathed.

"What time is your physical therapy done? Harper has us doing some sort of team building activity, but we should be finished by 1 p. m."

"Team-building?" He clutched the white shirt he was wearing and feigned surprise.

I chuckled. "I know. There's this one guy, Bryce. He's a total ass. I hate the way he talks to Harper. Like he questions everything she says. Now we're all forced to play nice as a team." I groused. "And it doesn't help that he thinks I got the job just because I know Harper," I told Chaquille about Bryce and what I had learned about nepotism.

"Don't let anyone make you feel bad about knowing people who can help you. Harper is your friend. I might call her a mentor, but I've seen the way she dresses." Chaquille gave a fake shudder. "He's probably just jealous, anyway."

Throwing my t-shirt over my head and running my fingers through my few inches of hair, I scoffed. "Jealous? Of what? I drive an Oldsmobile Cutlass that my dead grandfather gave me." Grateful to even have an internship was an understatement. Bryce couldn't possibly be jealous of me.

Chaquille's face softened. "Indy. You're smart. Fine. You have a way with words. You speak to a different side of me. Oh, and you used to have some booty." He teased. "The way your mind works... It's like there's so many parts of you, and they all turn me on." He leaned into my face and our foreheads touched. I breathed in his stank breath. But I didn't say anything. I didn't care.

"Chaquille . . ."

"Don't worry. I love you too." Chaquille searched my eyes for comfort. For confirmation.

I *comforted*. I *confirmed*.

A tear rolled down my face and before they dropped down onto my bare skin, Chaquille was already wiping it away.

A few minutes later, I dropped off Chaquille and promised to meet him for lunch as I made my way toward Synergy House. It sat off-campus, right outside Titus University property and the city just seemed to spring up out of nowhere. I checked out the tall buildings around me, while the blinker in The Bus dinged loudly. What was it like to live in the city? I mean, where Titus was located was in the city, but it was a college-town. This city had real life people working and bustling from place to place. The women wore pencils skirts with sneakers on and their heels tucked in a lunch bag to work in a skyscraper with no grass or water around. Were people happy here? I checked out the strangers who walked fast with their heads down. They didn't look up or nod at anyone. In Tunica Rivers, we greeted everyone on the street, and we talked about the weather non-stop. *'Does it look like rain? Check out that cloud over there?'* I had seen more than my share of rainbows from our backyard so many times I grew up thinking they only showed up in Tunica Rivers, and they were my special thing. I hadn't seen one since Ez.

A car beeped behind me as I jerked from my stupor and realized the light was green. I pulled into the parking lot and hustled inside so I wouldn't be late.

Bryce was usually first, then me, followed by Tristan or Kathleen. We always waited on Harper, who seemed to have

an aversion to anything related to the morning and being on time. When she bustled in with a long black trench-coat, platform shoes, and the largest cup of coffee I had ever seen. I rolled my eyes, already amused.

"How is everyone this morning? Great." She didn't wait for anyone to answer. "Kathleen, I thought we could start with your article this morning. The corrections you submitted were good, but I think we could make them better."

Kathleen shrunk into her chair as Harper wrote on the dry erase board with a red marker. I cringed, knowing the all too familiar sound of a red marker hitting a board in criticism of your work. "I liked how you combined mental health with recent events in Haiti. Totally see the correlation" Harper gave an exaggerated hand swipe and the bangles on her wrist jiggled. "But we have to make it palatable for all readers. Right now, the way it's written, it just sounds. . . Angry. Inflammatory even."

"Oh snap! She said, angry. Shot fired," Bryce snickered.

"Angry?" Kathleen whispered. She leaned back in her chair and chewed on the end of her pen. Her braids cascaded down her shoulders, framing her tawny and confused face.

"Yes, I mean. We can go through it together as a group. Remember, we give each-other constructive criticism not to hurt anyone's feelings, but to improve their writing. This is an excellent piece, Kathleen. We just have to tighten it up a bit." Harper danced in place when she said, *tighten*.

"It's okay, Kathleen. I'm up next to the slaughterhouse." Tristan chuckled.

Kathleen stood. "I'm going to the bathroom. I'll be right back." I watched her walk away and I grabbed the back of my neck, wondering if my chopped hair was long enough to put into braids.

A marked up dry erase board later, I was famished for lunch. Kathleen's criticism was actually constructive and when Bryce tried to take things in a mean-spirited direction, Harper reigned him back in. It was exhausting, but interesting. Once it was over, I plopped down into my seat across from Kathleen, who was typing away at her computer. She was clicking the keyboard fast and hard and didn't even flinch when I sat down. She was in a zone.

I took out my phone and texted Chaquille.

> **ME:** You ready for lunch? I'm starved!

> **CHAQUILLE:** My Mom is in town. She came down from NY to surprise me for my birthday! Do you mind if she comes too?

> **ME:** Of course not. I'll meet you at the Sushi spot in a few minutes.

Chaquille and I wanted to try this new Sushi spot in the city. Chaquille's birthday was a few days away, and I wondered why she didn't text me or call. Not that we were super close, but when Chaquille was in the hospital, it was me and her who set up camp by his bedside. For weeks, we alternated sleeping and eating in shifts to make sure someone was always there with him. His mom was strong, and by the looks of Chaquille's dad nowhere to be found, it was because she had no choice but to be. She was nice, but she always spoke with a hint of spice, like she could exchange her penny loafers for Timberland Boots any day.

"Indy. . . do you think this article is inflammatory?" Kathleen cleared her throat.

I looked up from my phone. "Anything about immigrants right now is inflammatory. It doesn't mean we shouldn't write about it."

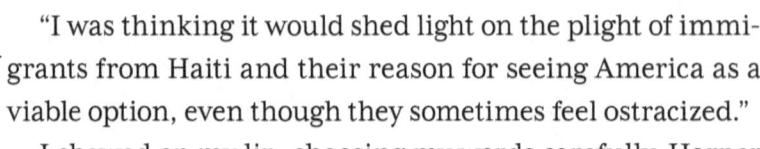

"I was thinking it would shed light on the plight of immigrants from Haiti and their reason for seeing America as a viable option, even though they sometimes feel ostracized."

I chewed on my lip, choosing my words carefully. Harper chopped down Kathleen's article, and while I agreed with some things Harper pointed out, we had one thing in common. We were writers, and we were sensitive about our shit.

"I think it's personal to you. Find a way to make sure they hear your voice, and still advocate for Haitians the way you want. It's a story that needs to be told, just maybe from a different point of view."

Kathleen nodded. "Yeah. . . you're right. From a different angle," she whispered.

I turned back to my computer and made sure to shut it down and sign out before meeting Chaquille for lunch. My article about grief glared back at me, only a few sentences long. Nepotism or not, I would make sure my shit was tight, and that included more than just these few words I mustered up.

I grabbed my jacket and waved my goodbyes, shooting Sidney a quick text message telling her I loved her. Three bubbles popped up and a simple, "Love you too" was her response. My heart sank. My chest was tight, and I pressed into my ribcage, wondering if I was having a heart attack or an anxiety attack. I couldn't really tell the difference, anyway.

I hustled across the lot to The Bus when I heard someone whistle, and it stopped me dead in my tracks.

I knew that whistle. I smelled her. I breathed for her.

I knew *her.*

Sonia Lewis barreled from behind a tree and scampered my way with a grin flashing across her face.

"My dear daughter! Isn't it a glorious day?! I told you we would see each other soon, and Mommy keeps her promises! Do you like my new outfit? I picked this up at the consignment shop in town. You know I went to King's house. You know Trochesse got them people following me? I'm smarter than them, though. Anyway, I went to King's house, and he gave me some money for clothes and a motel room, but he said that I can't stay and sent me on my way. He told me you were here, working at some big-time publishing house. I hitch-hiked all this way, girl. He didn't even let me see Sidney! That man is still looking good. Tall and fine, just like I remember him. I still wouldn't mind putting my shoes under his bed any day. He used to make me scream for Jesus Saturday night and then take me to see Him Sunday morning! Umph Umph umph! Anyway, I got me these nice threads. I'm supporting my girl." She modeled her outfit.

Mom rambled on as I stood there, mouth gaped open. "Mom. . . you came all this way? For me?" I studied my mom's bright yellow outfit. She wore a Titus University sweatsuit, ripped at the neck. It had soft fuzzies on it from being washed one too many times. She looked like the ultimate college parent. My mom was the type of person who always looked better heavy set and today she looked like she had missed no meals with the extra weight around her midsection, arms, and thighs. Her chocolate face was smooth, not a wrinkle in sight. Her real hair was stuffed under a short auburn wig. I examined the features of the woman I would look like in a few years.

"Yes, girl, why wouldn't I? You're my oldest daughter. I heard them talking about transferring me to some facility in New York. New York! Can you imagine? I hated that place when *The FatCats* used to tour there. So much noise and mean people." She shuddered. "Anyway. Can I come with you? I'm still hiding out from the people they sent to look for me. I know I can't stay with you, but where are you going? What are you doing? Can I come for a little while?" she asked with hesitant eyes.

I studied my mom. Her face. Her hair. Her clothes. Her outfit. Her smile. She broke out of Trochesse and tracked me down. Her oldest daughter. I gripped my car keys tighter in my hand and they were leaving indentations. My phone buzzed in my pocket, and I knew it was probably Chaquille wondering where I was for our lunch date. Meeting him and his mom seemed as far away as the moon right now. I had my own Mom to meet with, and her time was more pressing.

CHAPTER EIGHT

MOM SHOVED FRENCH fries in her mouth and slathered mayonnaise and ketchup on her sandwich. It made a weird orange color as it seeped through the sides of the bread. She licked her upper lip and her eyes never left the bun.

"This is a hook-up, Indy. When you're locked away for years, you have to get creative and make meals on your own," she explained. She stirred her water with a butter knife and the ice whirled in the glass, but not before she cleaned off all the silverware at the table. Twice. The diner we ducked into was a far cry from the sushi I planned to share with Chaquille and his mom. I shot him a quick text and let him know I couldn't make it.

"Where are you staying?" I peered at her. My stomach grumbled for food minutes ago but with my mom standing before me, I was hardly hungry anymore.

"I told you that King gave me some money so I could get me a motel. It's right outside of town. I figured I could stay with you, but I didn't want to intrude with your little boyfriends. How many you got now, anyway? I bet they eating right out the palm of your hands." She giggled like a schoolgirl, and it

made people around us turn to see what all the commotion was about.

"What are you worried about? Mind your business, you'll live longer!" Mom squawked.

"Mom, turn around!" I hissed. "Does Sidney know you're here? Does anyone know? Why didn't King tell me you came to the house?"

"You got potatoes in your ears, girl? I went to King's house to see Sidney. He lives the closest to Trochesse, and I figured it would be easier to get there than my daddy's house. I knocked on the door and I thought it was going to be like the movies, girl. He was going to swing the door open, look me up and down and see how those Trochesse pancakes went straight to these hips, and he scoops me up in a dip, and I would give him something he can feel like *EnVogue*."

Mom wiped her mouth and gazed out the window.

"I thought we were gonna be somebody rocking, knocking the boots. But he told me to leave. Said they hired some big-time detective to search for me and I couldn't stay because they would come looking for him. He said Sidney is going to live with him. You think he had a woman there? He ain't never passed me over for no porkers before!" she exclaimed.

"Shhh," I said, and motioned with my hands to lower her tone. Her pressured talking was too much to follow and the louder she got, the more heads turned our way. I peeked around the room at prying eyes, Mom's bright yellow get up, and her lopsided wig.

"Don't be embarrassed by me, girl, I'll snatch this wig off right now!" she huffed, and food shot out of her mouth and landed right in the center of my omelet.

"Sidney is not going to live with him. She's staying with us," I said with a firm head nod. I don't think Sidney knew that either, but she couldn't leave us. She just couldn't.

Mom wiped her mouth and gaped at me like she was seeing me for the first time. "My Indy-Lindy. All grown up and
standing up for her sister. Look at you, girl."

I inhaled and tried to control my breathing from the tears
that wanted to spill. I was standing up for Sidney, for Ez, for
Paisley. Shit—for me.

"What are you doing the rest of the day? Do you have a phone
or anything?" I checked her out and besides a few dollars she
kept flashing, she didn't look like she had anything with her.

"Oh naw, girl. I was hoping you could take me to a store so
I can get me one of those Obama phones. Are they still free?
It's been so long since I've had one." She stopped eating and
looked around like she just realized she was in a restaurant.
"Mam, have you any sherbet to cleanse my pallet?" She pulled
at the waitresses skirt and spoke in her English accent.

I closed my eyes and sighed. Meet my mom. The raging
schizophrenic.

"Sherbet?" the waitress repeated. She held a pot of hot coffee
in her hand, and she chomped on her gum like she didn't have
time for Mom's shit. "No, we don't have that. Sorry."

"Fine well bring me more wattaaa to cleanse my utensils
and mints to freshen my breath." Mom's accent was thick and
abusive. I winced and hurried to pay the bill.

Mom and I stopped at a convenience store where she ran in
to purchase her phone. My phone buzzed.

"Shit!" I fumed. Chaquille was calling. What would I say?
*"Hey there, Chaquille. My mom broke out of the looney bin and she's
back in town."* No one knew she was back yet except for King,
and I was sure he didn't tell Sidney. I couldn't tell anyone yet
either; I had to be sure she was safe.

"Hello?" I breathed. I tried to give my best, unassuming voice.

"Indy? What happened? We waited for an hour before I got your text. I called you over and over? Are you alive?"

Chaquille's concern was endearing and warmed my heart. Feeling guilty, I swallowed. "Uh. . . yea. I'm fine. I caught a flat leaving work and left my phone in the car as they changed my tire. I'm okay," I lied. And I felt bad, boy–did I feel bad.

"Are you sure? I mean. I called over and over?" Chaquille questioned.

"No, everything is fine. Is your mom with you?"

"Yeah, she's right here."

"Hiii, Indy! Missed you at lunch!" Chaquille's mom screamed in the background.

"Hey!" I shouted back, and it was as fake as could be because I really wanted to run my finger down a chalkboard or something. I wanted to go to lunch with Chaquille and his mom. I *wanted* Chaquille, and his mom. Instead, I was lying to them. The deception sat in the pit of my stomach, knotted and twisted.

"I'll see you later. We're going to head to the mall or something. I'll catch up with you later. . . Okay?" Chaquille said, riddled with concern.

I spied Mom rushing out of the store with a small bag. An older gentleman held the door for her and she twirled around in front of him and winked at him over her shoulder.

"Okay." I nodded into the phone and pressed end.

"You can take me to the motel. I'm gonna catch me a catnap and then I'll call you later so we can game plan."

"Game plan?" I scrunched my face.

"Yes girl! About what to do about Ez."

"How did they tell you?" I asked in a whisper. Curiosity got the best of me. I saw what they did to Ez firsthand, but I wondered how she received the news from Trochesse.

"One of those ugly nurses sent me down to one of the social workers, and they told me. Just said it so cold and flat. I wanted to smack her right across her damn face," Mom fumed.

After I dropped off Mom, I texted Harper and told her I wouldn't be back at work in the afternoon. I just couldn't. My mom was out and on the run from Trochesse. I was harboring a fugitive and as much as I hated this, I would *always* harbor her—fugitive or not.

See you tonight at the pub for happy hour? Harper texted back. Before we broke for lunch, she invited everyone to a bar for another team building charade. I didn't think it was the smartest idea. Bryce hailed all the way from Texas, where everything was bigger and better he claimed. He was already twenty-one and so was Tristan. It was Kathleen and I, who were technically still underage.

"Oh fooey," Harper snorted loudly. "You'll just have to get virgin drinks." She giggled.

I wasn't in the mood to play nice with Tristan, Bryce, and Kathleen—not after seeing Mom. I took off all my clothes, and I hopped in the bed, pulling my body pillow into me and hugging it tightly. Mom said we needed to talk about what to do about Ez. What did that mean? It was so much to think about and soon, my eyes were heavy.

When I woke, Ez had made his way to my dreams again. He was grilling food at his house on Tunica Rivers. *'Keep the house, Indy. Seal it with love,'* he fussed. Whatever that meant.

I grabbed my phone and checked the time. If I was meeting the team for drinks, I would need to be ready in one hour.

After a quick shower and a hair wash, I added curl cream and ran my fingers through my mane, hoping that it would

coif into tiny little ringlets. I tossed on my jacket and grabbed my keys before I dialed the number Mom gave me for her burner phone.

No answer.

I texted Dad:

> **ME:** Hey, Dad. has anyone heard from Mom? Any news on the detective?

> **DAD:** Nope, nothing, honey. Last I heard, the detective was still looking for her and she's still on the lam. Look at little miss Paisley!

Dad sent a picture of Paisley passed out asleep in his lap. He was grinning from ear to ear.

I beamed.

CHAPTER NINE

PULLED UP IN front of The PaddyWagon and saw Harper out front waiting for us to arrive. She wore a full men's suit jacket and a matching vest. Her pins adorned the lapel and from here, she appeared to be sparkling. I checked my phone once more, waiting for Mom to call back before I headed inside.

"What a way to start out the weekend! Drinks with the team! Now this is what I call bonding." Harper giggled and did a little jig.

Thursday night was bustling with activity in The Paddy-Wagon as police officers convened with large mugs of fuzzy beer. American flags littered the walls with pictures of past presidents shaking hands with people, who looked more important than me. Harper picked the perfect place to meet as a group. It was in the lion's den, but she said all the important people at Synergy House converged there. I clenched my fists and thought about Ez and the way the police disregarded his life and left him slain on his own property. This was part of the reason Sidney *had* to stay at the house. Protecting her would be easier when she was on our turf.

I ordered a soda and sat down at an open table across from Harper and Tristan, who were already knocking back a few drinks. Slurping my fizzies, the door chimed and Kathleen sauntered into the building. She did a double take as she noticed the police officers surrounding her.

"What's all this about?" she mused, sitting down across from me.

"Hey, there's no sitting down. We are here to get to know each other as a team! Come up to the bar!" Harper fussed.

"No, it's okay, Harper. I don't want anything." Kathleen waved her hands, but Harper was too busy leaned over the counter barking out non-alcoholic beverages to the flustered bartender like they were the real thing.

I took in the sights around me and eyed the officers. Were any of them killers? They trained for things like that, they actually sat down in a classroom and were taught how to handle a threat. They used words like *subdue, neutralize, restrain.* All words that stung and left me grandfather-*less.* They were killers. They had killed Ez. I sipped my soda to calm my nerves. I tried not to breathe deeply as the pain sharpened in my chest. I wonder why Harper picked this bar out of them all.

The other half of the team arrived, and Bryce breezed into the room. He looked around and smiled at officers and shook hands with a few. He didn't do a double take like Kathleen and I did.

"Hey ya'll, what are we drinking? Well, I guess, what are me and Tristan drinking?" He chuckled.

"That's what I am talking about!" Harper slapped Bryce's back a little harder than I thought necessary.

Kathleen cringed too.

"So now that we are all here, let's learn more about each other! Tristan? You go first!" Harper urged.

Tristan was sipping from a large cup of something dark, and when Harper said his name, he gulped.

"Umm. Okay, I'll go first then. I'm Tristan. You guys know that already. I'm in grad school. From Louisiana, like most of you." He waved his hands around like he didn't know what else to say. "Just trying to get through my time at Synergy House and one day, become a journalist with CNN." His tossed hair framed his face, and his eyes were dark and piercing.

"My man, speak for yourself. I am not from Louisiana! Texas is the best!" Bryce jumped in. He gulped from his glass. "Anyway, you know me. I am Bryce, also in grad-school and I've got big plans for Synergy House. I might own it one day and be your boss, and the ladies can write the recipes column," he snickered.

Tristan and Kathleen chuckled, and I wondered what was so funny.

"I'm Indigo, but you can call me Indy. I'm also from Louisiana too and I am a writer. Undergrad."

Short and sweet.

"I am Kathleen. I was in school for nursing, but I changed my major to broadcast journalism. Undergrad," Kathleen said. She picked at lint on her sweater as she spoke.

"Marvelous!" Harper beamed. "My team, I know that we already know one another, but we sometimes have to be reminded that we are on the same team and we work together. I've set up a few more team building events throughout the year. Harper stuffed a few peanuts on the table in her mouth. "I have a few new pieces to highlight on campus. One of them is about the Wellness Center. . ." Harper talked, but conversation around me drowned the sounds out in my brain.

Chestnut. Someone had said the word, *Chestnut.*

I peered up front and two officers sitting in a booth in front of us were conversing. "They still have found nothing relating

to a disappearance. I'm telling you, Frank. Something ain't right. I think the wife had something to do with it," he said.

The other officer leaned back in his chair and palmed his chin, and my eyes darted everywhere but on him as I sat across from him in the booth. "Maybe it was one of those girls he was messing with. I didn't know there were so many. You think one of them killed him? That's my hunch!"

"Imagine being killed for fish! Must've been a big fish!" He giggled and together, the officers hollered and slapped at their knees.

'They'll never find the fish bones, right, Indy?' a voice in me whistled. Was I afraid? No. Was I scared? Yes. I didn't want to hurt anyone that I loved. But Mr. Chestnut hurt those that I loved. I smirked and tried to not look like I was paying them any attention, but they were right. They were so right. It was a big fish. I was the biggest.

"Indy? Indy?" Harper interrupted. Tristan, Kathleen, and Bryce were gazing at me.

"Oh! Uh yes? The Wellness Center." I hadn't heard a thing. The conversation in front of us was way better.

"Good. Then I can mark you down for it?" Harper quizzed.

I hadn't even turned in a good article when she asked me the first time. I mean, it was workable, and it needed heavy editing, which Harper took upon herself to make the corrections, but it wasn't my best work. It was enough to keep me afloat in a paid internship. Harper didn't care how bad it was. She wanted me to showcase my skills.

"You can mark me down for it." I nodded.

"Great! I think highlighting the Wellness Center and the good work they do on campus will show the board of directors how mental health awareness is sorely lacking at the school."

Harper was assigning work in a bar on a Thursday night.

"Do we need to talk about this now? I have an interview set up with someone from the Chestnut case," Bryce questioned. He glanced at his watch, now in a hurry. His eyes were on a tall, leggy blonde who had just walked into the bar.

"I have a few more ideas for specific things I would like each of you to work on. Kathleen, I think we can move forward with your piece about Haiti. Tristan and Bryce, I have a piece about off campus housing. I think you both would be great for. Bryce is working hard on his piece about Coach Chestnut. Anyway, we have time for all of that! But tonight, let's have fellowship!" Harper chugged a drink. "Do any of you like martinis? They have a Banana Foster Martini that is to die for! Of course, yours will be a virgin drink, ladies. But you must try it. It is divine!"

"Martini? Martinis are for the ladies." Bryce crossed his arms. "And besides, I am allergic to bananas."

"Allergic to bananas. How is someone allergic to bananas?" Kathleen laughed, and it was the first time I had seen her break into a genuine smile. She had an enormous gap in between her two front teeth that was so cute, I wondered why she didn't smile more often.

Bryce's ears turned red, and he shuffled his feet under the table. "Yeah man. I don't know what it is. I have to keep my inhaler and an epi-pen with me everywhere." He shrugged.

"This shit is BANANAS! B-A-N-A-N-A-S!" Harper sang as she lifted Kathleen to her feet and began two stepping with her in front of the bar. It paralyzed Kathleen with fear, but after much coaxing from Harper, she laughed and moved her waist.

"You get up here too, Indy!" Harper squealed. I was going back home to Tunica Rivers for the weekend, and Dad and I were riding out to another rental property he was scoping out. I checked my phone and saw a few text messages from Mom's new phone before clicking it away and joining Harper.

> **MOM:** Are you coming to see me?

> **MOM:** What are you doing?

> **MOM:** How do I get Netflix in here?

> **MOM:** What is your account info?

Mom shot off four different messages back-to-back.

How fitting. The voices had finally given me a break and weren't coming in at warp's speed anymore, but Mom's real-life messages were. I read each of them and sighed before clicking my phone off and making a mental note to call her back when I left the bar. I also made a mental note to call King. I got up and danced with Kathleen and Harper.

CHAPTER TEN

"**B**RYCE CAME AND interviewed some of us. I didn't know what to say, so I just told him I thought he was right about his theory and that something fishy happened. He seemed to like that. I know how you feel about it already, but girl I think this could end up on *Investigation Discovery* or something," Theodora whispered. I turned down the street, gritting my teeth into the phone. Something fishy sure did happen to Mr. Chestnut.

"Theodora, that kid is bad news, watch yourself around him." The side of my head throbbed. When Bryce said he had interviews lined up I didn't think he meant the track team. That would make sense though, he was the track coach and spent all his time with them. But still, Bryce was getting a little too close for comfort now, and I hated hearing his name escape Theodora's lips.

"You keep saying that but you're still not saying anything. Bad news how, Indy?"

I paused as the trees whipped by me in the window. "I can't explain it. It's just a feeling. Intuition, I guess."

Theodora sighed. "Okay, Indy, we'll just agree to disagree." I wasn't sure what we were disagreeing about but I bit my tongue. Why wouldn't she just listen to me?

I parked my car and tried not to sound annoyed as we said our goodbyes. "Theodora, I'm here. I'll call you later."

We were not on the same page about Mr. Chestnut. The more I tried to put it behind me and forget about the whole thing, Bryce was interviewing the team members and fueling Theodora's conspiracy theories. Why didn't she just believe me? I was her friend, not Bryce.

Knocking on the door, my stomach was in knots as I tried to shake the conversation with Theodora.

Mila.

She was my best friend all throughout grade school. Even after she and my ex-boyfriend, Malachi, began dating; Mila held a piece of my heart that drew me back in and had me lightly rapping on her door early this Saturday morning. The last time I saw her was at a random gas station in town. It was an icy conversation—one that still never sat right with me. It was random as hell, but I missed her.

"Hey. . . Indy," Mila said, holding the door wide. She smiled, and it was the same smile that comforted me throughout grade school. I pulled at the bottom of my jacket and concentrated on controlling my breathing.

"Hey Mila. I was just in town and figured I would stop by and see you. I hope this isn't weird." I cringed inside. It was weird.

"Come inside," she said. Mila's house was a double-wide widow trailer. The furniture was old-style with lots of wood and her mom still kept those plastic runners over the floors that held daggers in the bottom if they ever caught onto your feet. There were small holes in some walls but Mila's Mom strategically placed end tables there so they weren't noticeable.

The house smelled like chicken. They weren't living the high life but were making do with what they had.

"Where's your mom?" I ran my hand through my hair.

"Your braids, Indy. Your hair. I don't remember the last time I've seen you without braids." Mila examined my hair. She held out her hand to instinctively touch them, but she stopped herself and gazed at my face.

"I know." I palmed the back of my neck. "Trying something new, I guess. A lot has been going on."

"I know." She nodded. "I am so sorry to hear about Ez. Malachi and I came to the funeral, but I didn't want to intrude, so we stayed in the back."

My head shot up. "You did?"

"Of course, Indy. We were best friends practically all of our lives. I will always try to be there for you." Mila's long, jet black hair fell over her face and she brushed it out of the way. She wiped her face from where I thought a tear was falling.

"Mila. . . about your grandmother. She passed away last year. I'm sorry I didn't make it. There was a lot going on. . . with me. I'm sorry. I'm sorry for all of it."

"I'm sorry too." Mila nodded, and this time, I was sure. A tear had escaped her eye. I slid over to Mila and grabbed her in a long hug. So many memories, years, tears, and dramas between us. She was missed—my friend. We were both crying when Mila's front door opened and her mom barreled in carrying grocery bags. "Indy," she breathed.

"Hi Ms. Davis." I stood and embraced her. The same woman who fed me and took me into her home when I needed a reprieve from mine.

"I am so glad you are back. She's missed you." Ms. Davis whispered into my ear. "Now ya'll come help me get the rest

of the groceries out of this car. Mila. Did you tell Indy about the baby?"

My neck jerked around as I studied Mila's body. Behind the simple white t-shirt and black tights she wore, I found the small imprint of a baby bump. Mila was always thick for a white girl and she had curved for days. But now her shape was more. . . feminine.

"Are you. . . pregnant?" I motioned to her stomach with my nose.

"Guilty." She gave a sheepish smile. "Malachi and I have a little person coming in about five months." Mila touched her stomach.

"Congratulations. . . I am so happy for you guys," I said through clenched teeth. I wasn't sure why but I wanted those words to mean so much more to me than they did.

"It wasn't the plan, you know. I'm still living here with Mom and working at Dr. Rasner's office. But Malachi is really doing it big! He got the head chef position at La Auberge in Tunica Rivers. People come from far away to try out some of his dishes. We're getting our own place soon, and waiting for bambina to arrive." She smiled and touched her stomach again.

She had the pregnancy glow, and I hadn't noticed it before when she opened the door. Her skin was shiny. When we were in school, I had filled out college applications for her and helped her apply. When she didn't get in, she opted to work in town at a doctor's office with her mom, and if I was honest, I resented it. Mila was smart. She had the gift of the gab and people liked her. I didn't want her to waste her talents by staying in Tunica Rivers when she could do so much more, but looking at her today, I was wrong.

Mila was happy. She was living the life that she wanted, and now she and Malachi would be parents. Just because this wasn't my story didn't mean it was the wrong story. A golf-ball sized lump of guilt sat in my throat. I was eating crow, as Ez would say. I had pulled away from my friends because their choices differed from mine.

"But you had a lot going on," a voice in my head said. *"Don't be so hard on yourself."*

But I was. I was hard on myself. Trying to run from the voices and manage everything had taken its toll in ways that I hadn't realized were important to me. People my age were around me maturing, working full-time jobs, and starting families. I had the voices and a murderous history to contend with. I thought about Will, and our friendship or relationship that never was. I loved Chaquille. He spoke to parts of me that were yet to be revealed. But damn. . . Will was parts of me too. He and I were united in a way that had to be mended, no matter how angry he still was. I had to make our friendship right. I *would* make our friendship right.

Mila and I talked for another hour. We laughed at our old Tunica Rivers yearbook and giggled about our former class-mates. Tears and ugly cries escaped us when remembering Ez. We hugged and vowed to keep in touch. I didn't know if it was true or not, but I would try, and I hoped she would, too.

After spending a few hours with Dad checking out new prop-erties, I headed back to school with a box of Ez's old things in tow. He was interested in purchasing a third property closer to my school because he said it was easy money. College students always needed off campus housing, and if I was closer to the property, I could help manage it. I didn't know how I would manage an entire house when I couldn't manage myself.

I pulled out my phone to see if Mom called. She didn't. I started to shoot King a quick text message, asking him to

call me and before I could, Mom's number finally flashed across my screen. Finally. I called her three times already that morning.

"Mom. . . are you okay?" I demanded.

"Girl, I am just fine. Where are you at? What are you doing? I was staying at this shelter and I had this man make me a fake ID, so those people from Trochesse can't track me. I am officially Bethany Lightfoot." Mom cackled into the phone. "Anyway, I am around your campus. Where are you? Do you want to grab something to eat?"

As much as I tried not to, I smiled into the phone. "We can grab something. You can come up to my room. The security is lax on the weekends and I can sneak you in. Make sure you have your fake ID on you. And Mom. Please behave."

"Behave, girl, don't be telling me to behave. You behave! All I hear is what I see! I'll see you in a flash!"

When I pulled up to my dorms, I spotted Mom sitting at a picnic table across from the dorm building. She wore a black trench coat and a fedora hat.

"My Indy Lindy," she complained and grabbed my waist. "Look at these hips, here. You got these birthing hips, just like me and your Mama Jackie, girl. Don't be giving birth, though. Not yet." She wagged her finger and embraced me.

I held my mom tight around the neck and inhaled her scent. She smelled like home. I closed my eyes and remembered Ez and Mama Jackie—up there together, smiling at me and Mom. I took brain pictures of it all.

Mom was extra sweet to the security guard while I signed her name into the visitor's log. The student security guard, who sat there on the weekends, didn't even look up from his

magazine. I had to be extra careful when I was writing Bethany Lightfoot and choked back a giggle at the name.

"Have a nice day!" Mom said to the guard in her English accent. I tugged at her arm and pulled her down the hallway as the guard gave her a raised eyebrow.

"They call this a dorm room?" Mom looked around in disgust. I had two twin beds pushed together to make one. The walls were cold and cinderblock and the floors were old parkay.

"Welcome to my home, away from home." I waved my hands around.

"And where is that boyfriend of yours? I'd love to meet him? What's his name, again?"

"Chaquille, Mom."

"Chaquille? Like that fat head basketball player? Who would name their child such a thing?"

"Well, you named me Indigo."

"Indigo is a color. A beautiful expression of the sunset. Don't be ashamed of your name, Indy Lindy. It was Ez approved."

I held my breath and sank onto my bed. "Ez liked the name?"

Mom nodded. "Sure did. He said, *'I ain't never heard no such kind of name. . . But I reckon I like it.'*"

I cracked my neck. I dug through the box that Dad gave me and I remembered Ez's things inside. "These are all Ez's," I said. "Dad gave them to me."

Mom and I glanced at each other and paused before peering into the box. We found old t-shirts, CDs, pictures of Ez when he was in the service, and his dog tags. He looked so young and thin. A wide, silly grin spread across his face, and I saw Sidney in his eyes. Mom and I were quiet as we examined each memory, each piece of Ez with heavy hearts. When we settled onto the DVDs, I popped them into my laptop. Dad had a few home videos of Ez converted and transferred to the DVDs. The first one was Ez with a guitar, singing a blues song

to Mama Jackie. The sight of both in their prime stopped me and Mom in our tracks. Mom sat down on the bed beside me and fat tears rolled down her face.

"*I needs me a woman, and it's this woman right here. My Juju love. My juju love,*" Ez sang. Mama Jackie giggled and swatted Ez away with her dish towel. Their love was so genuine. Ez's autism didn't matter. Mom's mental health didn't matter. They were all love. I held my breath as I watched them move in sync.

"Those officers did this to us. Tunica Rivers did this to us. They didn't believe us, nor try to help us with Ez. They so easily killed him. They can't get away with this!" Mom fumed.

We were on the same page in the same chapter in the same book.

"No, they can't." I nodded.

"They have to pay. They took him from us. He still had time." Mom cried. She held my body pillow to her chest and squeezed until it was deformed.

I wiped my face and paused the video, the memories too much for me. "What should we do, Mom?"

"We'll take them out, one by one. Everyone who's involved in Ez's death. They will pay!" She banged her hand on the wall behind her. For the first time in a long time, I agreed with my mom. They took one of mine, so *we* would take one of theirs.

CHAPTER ELEVEN

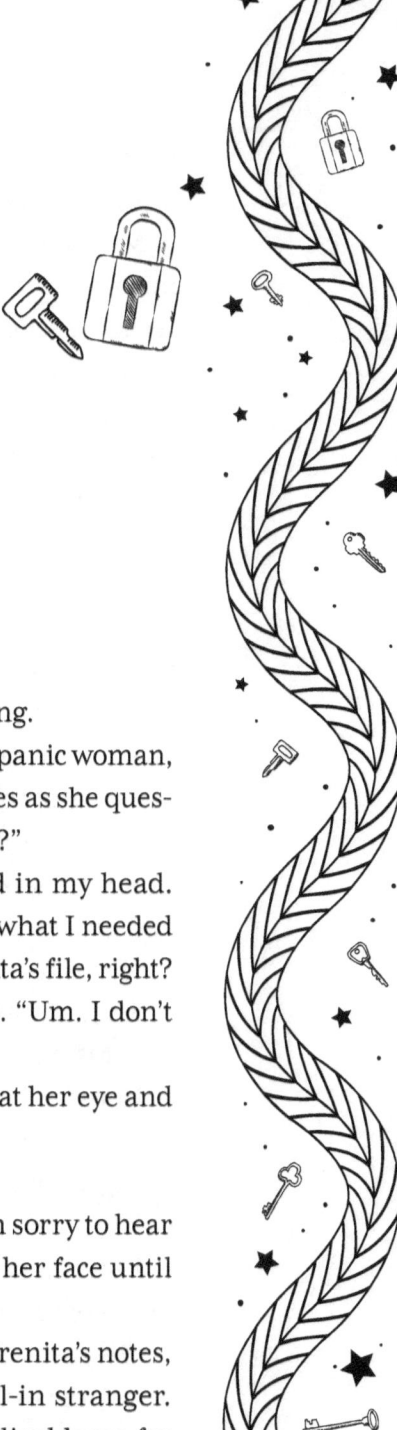

WE SAT ACROSS from each other, staring.

Trenita's replacement was an older Hispanic woman, and she swayed back and forth in circles as she questioned me. "What would you like to talk about?"

What would you *like to talk about?* I repeated in my head. Wasn't *she* the counselor? Shouldn't she know what I needed to talk about? She would have read that in Trenita's file, right?

I cleared my throat and crossed my ankles. "Um. I don't know. My grandfather just died. . ."

"Yes, I read that." Ms. Ramos began picking at her eye and blinking like something was bothering her.

"Are you okay?"

"I'm fine, just have something in my eye. I'm sorry to hear that. How did he pass?" Ms. Ramos rubbed at her face until her skin was red.

I knew the *how* he passed was definitely in Trenita's notes, and I wasn't about to rehash it with some fill-in stranger. Trenita and I had been preparing for her medical leave for weeks and I knew it was coming. She already introduced

me to this Ms. Ramos before her departure, but I still wasn't feeling this lady or her eye.

Ms. Ramos dug through her purse and whipped out a pocket mirror and picked at her eye, blinking fast. "Indy, give me one second. I seem to have lint or something in my eye."

Indigo. . . I mulled. "Call me Indigo." I clasped my hands together and waited, already in checked out mode. I just could not find a decent therapist these days. They all seemed to irritate me, and it didn't take long to prove how I was just another number.

"Indigo. . ." Ms Ramos repeated. "Anyway. Where were we?"

She sat down and her eye was beet red now. She was trying to remain professional, but her eye was puffy. She looked like a blowfish and before I knew it, I giggled. Her mouth fell open, and with her eyes bulging, I laughed even harder. I held the sides of the couch and continued to crack up and before long, Ms. Ramos laughed too. "I'm so sorry. It's my allergies. Do I look crazy, Indigo?" Ms. Ramos clenched her stomach and chuckled.

"Just a tad bit. Don't worry, I'm a little crazy too."

Ms. Ramos and I snickered together. We would see about this, Ms. Ramos. We would see.

Hours earlier, I dropped mom off at the city park. I was worried that Minko Forrest was lurking around some corner, ready to jump out and scream *aha* at any moment. When I swung back by the park after my session with Ms. Ramos, she was standing in front of ducks and feeding them torn pieces of bread.

"Hey Ma." I walked beside her.

"Hi, my Indy Lindy." She smiled and leaned her head on my shoulder. She wore my thick Titus University sweater and the largest pair of tights that I could find in my dresser.

"What are you out here doing?" The water glistened under ducks gliding through the water.

"I'm talking to the water. About Mama Jackie and Ez."

"What did they say?" I followed her gaze.

"Oh, nothing, and everything." She tossed more bread. She hummed, and Mom's sweet voice carried through the water. The ducks quacked and move closer to us. I couldn't quite place the tune Mom was humming, but it sounded familiar. She cupped my chin and sang, "because when I love, I love, and I love some more. . ."

Ez wasn't much of a dancer, but he could hold a tune and sang his heart to Mama Jackie, and this song that she hummed was one of his favorites. The blues fed Ez's soul with words that he could never formulate.

I wondered how it felt to lose both parents in a matter of years, and each time they went away, you couldn't touch them, feel them, or love them one last time? Was that why Sidney wanted to leave us and live with her dad? Was she worried about losing a parent since, technically, she kind of sort of lost Mom, too? I bet Mom didn't see it that way. She believed herself to love out loud and often, even in her absence. It was funny how she still saw herself as an active parent, even locked away. But she was here now, though. Making up for lost time. Not that Sidney was here to see any of it, nor was she even allowed to know that Mom was here with me, feeding ducks and singing in the park in the middle of the day. I could keep the secret of Mom being home, but could Sidney? The more I thought about it, it made sense. King knew Sidney wouldn't be able to *not* tell someone her mom was back, so it was better if she didn't know at all.

I glanced at Mom's face and felt guilty for having this time with her that Sidney so desperately needed, too.

"Indy. Do you remember what I asked you? Last year when you came to see me at Trochesse?"

My fingers went numb and squeezed my knees. Mom asked me about my first kill. She didn't say his name, but she asked about Jaxon. Did she. . . remember that? Sucking in a deep breath.

"Yes, Mom. I remember."

"And how was it?" She dropped her head and cut her sneaky eyes at me.

"It was. . . necessary. . . it felt. . . like the right thing to do," I admitted.

"Humph. Serves them right. Serves them all right." She nodded like she had figured out the secret to life. And just like that—it was over. "Oh Indy! How was your doctor's appointment? Are you on the pill, my girl? Are you going to let me meet this boyfriend of yours? What are we doing for lunch? I thought we could go shopping for some clothes today?"

"It wasn't a doctor's appointment. It was a counseling session. And it was okay."

"Counseling! My girl! Are they pouring the water on your head until you tell them things? You know they blame the mother for everything, right? Everything!" Mom hopped in place and threw bread at the ground like a toddler. "Hey? Have you ever had fried duck? It's divine!" she said, chasing around a squawking duck.

I ignored Mom's comment about the duck. "They didn't put water on my head, Mom. It's not bad. Have you gone before?" I tipped my head up and looked at her. Were they doing that to her in Trochesse? Waterboarding her?

Mom changed the subject in the blink of an eye. "Do you want to go to the consignment shop? Yes! Let's go right now! You can get some wonderful second-hand pieces there. I only need about twenty dollars! How much money you got? Your daddy gave you a credit card or anything?" Mom shot out questions as we strolled back to the car.

When I fired up The Bus, she roared to life and Prince echoed from the speakers. Mom rolled down the window, and the wind whipped through her short hair. She shouted every word of the song out of the window and sang like it was Showtime at the Apollo. We sped through a green light and passed an older man hobbling down the street with a cane. Mom's neck swung around while she looked him up and down.

"You know, he looks like that man they say I ran over!" She cackled.

'She said, 'they said,' a voice in my head giggled.

Mom said it as if they didn't have her on camera from at least four different angles. "Well, did you?" I pushed. Mom and I never discussed why she hit that man in her car, thus ending her time with us and beginning her doomed sentence in Trochesse.

"You never tell a man the truth, Indy. They just use it against you later, anyway." She pointed her finger in my face. "Just like King. You never show your whole hand. You take what you want. And I want my children. Now let's plan for Ez. How should we do this? Should we go to the station like Bonnie and Clyde? Should we make a video and hold someone for ransom? You know, I've been watching Chicago Fire. Maybe we should take they asses out with a big ol' fire! Or maybe we'll chop them up into small pieces. Yeah, that will give them a piece of my mind!" Mom giggled.

My shoulders sat so high they were almost touching my ears. Mom was talking about fire. I gripped the wheel until my knuckles turned white. "When I was in high school, there was this boy. He was threatening me. . . he wanted to blackmail me. . . and. . . and I killed him, Mom. I set him on fire."

79

I needed to talk about it. I had to bring it back up. I needed her focus back on me—even if for just a second. My knuckles were aching, so I loosened my grip. If I wasn't already sitting down, I was sure my knees would've buckled. My mouth was dry as hell and I searched the car for an old water bottle or something I could suck down quickly. But I felt lighter. Damn, I felt lighter. I cocked my head at my mom and waited for her to say something, anything.

The brightest smile spread across her face. A look that was like the one Dad gave me the day I graduated from high school. The same face he gave Paisley weeks ago when she was first born. Was Mom... dare I say it... proud?

"My Indy Lindy. . . I knew you would find your superpower. How did it feel?" She turned her body toward me in the car, facing me straight away like this was the first time she was hearing me say this. In some ways it was, I guess. Since she was a different person every day. Her short hair was all over her head from the wind and she cinched my Titus sweater at her neck. With her ghastly smile, she looked like a crazy old woman.

"Exhilarating. Terrifying. All at the same time," I confessed, darting my eyes between Mom and the road.

"Did anyone see you? That's where I went wrong. Too many people saw me. But shit, I didn't care. At least I think I didn't care. I really don't remember, it was so long ago. But that's what I'm talking about, Indy! We take down the man. No one hurts us and gets away with it! We have to teach Sidney to be strong. I have to get to her!" Mom banged on the window. "Come on, are you gonna let me borrow some money?" Mom's face morphed and her eyes darkened. She turned into someone more like herself.

"Mom, the man you hurt didn't hurt you, though." I ignored her money comment. I had exactly twenty dollars that

Chaquille gave me earlier for lunch, but man, I had my mom, and right now that was all the riches I needed.

"Doesn't matter, he's a man. He probably already did something to someone in his life he needed to atone for." She sat up straight, snorted, and smacked her hands together.

I thought about Jaxon, Mr. Chestnut, and the other man, wasting away in the bottom of a lake. Had they already done things they needed to atone for? Fuck yeah. My thoughts drifted to Chaquille. He was a man. But he had done nothing he needed to atone for. At least not to me. I mean, he was jumped last year on some bullshit. Was that his atonement? Or was that karma? And who was the keeper of atonement and karma, anyway? According to Theodora, Bryce was still conducting his track teams interviews and the more she talked about Mr. Chestnut, the more she believed that something happened to him, and it wasn't an act of karma. According to *her* standards, at least.

Like she would know a killer when she saw one.

I wasn't just a killer, nor a regular person. I was sandwiched somewhere between. Bad men had done things to me and people that I cared about, and for that, they had to pay. I didn't think about the other man that I killed, but I shuddered, remembering his gaze over my body, and the way his eyes rested on my wet t-shirt. He sealed his fate with me with one glance and a couple of ill-placed flirty words. He needed to atone. Sometimes I even forgot that I killed him, too.

But my dreams remembered.

He came to me in my dreams, just like Ez now. Mom jiggled in the car and danced to Prince when she rolled her window all the way down.

"Don't worry, my girl. We will come up with something for those dear old cops who killed our Ez. It is their turn to pay. And we'll get Sidney too!" She stuck out her hand and motioned

for me to shake it. When I did, she said, "Right on, my oldest child! Indy Lindy with the short hair. Why did you cut your braids, anyway? You looked so pretty with them. Now you look like me, with my neck out!" She rubbed the back of her neck and chuckled.

My lips parted, and a slow smile crept to my face. "They felt too heavy. I want to feel lighter."

CHAPTER TWELVE

THEODORA, NAOMI AND I were buried deep in our books. The Titus University library was tucked away in a corner of the campus covered by old trees which were there longer than I had been alive. Their shady presence made the building cold from lack of sunlight. I shivered in my seat and gazed out of the window past my laptop. I wondered what Mom was doing. As the days went on, we spent more time together, but I couldn't help but look over my shoulder wherever I was, waiting for Minko Forrest to cart her off back to Trochesse or somewhere worse. Where was worse, anyway? A world with no Ez and Mama Jackie was already worse, and I couldn't think of a single thing that could top that. I hoped she was okay.

I was deep in my thoughts this morning. Sidney was still quiet, and I was unsure how to get through to her. I texted her every morning before school and the energy was different. She wanted to leave us and the way I saw it, she wasn't allowed. But I still wanted her to be happy and at least talk to her about it. I texted King a few days ago and he never responded. I was

going home to Tunica for a visit and I made a mental note to stop by his house. We had business to discuss.

"Are you finished?" Theodora questioned, interrupting my thoughts.

It was my idea to meet with the girls for weekly study dates, but I was always the one distracted.

"I'm done." I sighed, pushing my laptop away from the table. It was a loaner from Naomi's Mom. I was walking in a daze one day from class and I tripped and fell with my old laptop in my hands. I was grateful to have this old clunker.

"Well, let's hear it, Robin Roberts." Naomi turned in her chair and closed the book. A large diamond ring flashed on her finger, and I wanted to ask her about it, but I bit my tongue.

My article about the Wellness Center was finished, but I was nervous about reading it to them. I chewed on the end of my pen until it was mangled and then I switched to scratching at the back of my neck. I just could not get used to myself as a bald-headed scallywag these days. Patience surely was a virtue, and I waited patiently for my hair to grow out before putting it back into braids.

"Shut up!" I threw a piece of paper at Naomi. She leaned over and caught it with her fist before giggling. "Okay, here it goes," I said.

Titus University Wellness Center: Friend or Foe?

As a freshman student, I visited the Titus University Wellness Center, hoping they would hear my story, listen to my concerns, and I would leave with a solid plan. Maybe even a little homework assignment or two. What I found was a series of mishaps and misunderstandings. The therapists at the Wellness Center are engaging in their own way, but

they should make more efforts to build strong relationships and rapport, right from the beginning. If the goal of each session is to promote wellness, well that needs to happen quicker so more students can access the mental health services they need.

What I learned throughout this process is if they assign you a therapist and it's not a good fit, don't give up. Look at the various bread companies in the grocery store. There are dozens (no pun intended) selling the same thing, and yet there is enough to appeal to everyone. If your first therapist doesn't appeal to you, try another one until you feel comfortable. Once I found my baker, we made our own delicious bread and have been rolling ever since!

When I finished reading, I shrugged and closed my laptop.

"Indy, that's great! You said you were having trouble coming up with something? What are you talking about?" Naomi tugged at the bottom of my sweater with a frown.

"I don't know if I want to put myself out there like that. Plus, Harper wants a positive spin on the Wellness Center, and my experience hasn't always been that. What will people think if they know I've gone to the Wellness Center? And that I've tried out more than one therapist? They'll think I'm nuts," I scoffed.

"You are a little nuts! We all are!" Theodora hissed. The librarian gave her a stern look. Her fishtail braid swung wildly behind her. "Listen, girl. You're a writer. You got away from it last year, but this is your time! We finally get to see you in action; you always told us how much you loved to write. You are a talented girl; and finally putting a face to the best well-kept secret on campus, and it's that these therapists are there for a reason. For a reason. You are not the only one going there; there wouldn't be so many of them if that were

the case." Theodora stood over me, waving her hands. A vein in her head was popping.

"And you need to let someone in," Naomi said.

"What does that mean?" I asked.

Theodora and Naomi shared a quick glance. Theodora spoke first. . . "Well, Indy. You go through a lot of things. We all do. But. . . you keep yours quiet. You can't keep holding everything in like this. This is why you have us." Her voice rose and she banged on the table.

The librarian was making her way toward us when Naomi said, "Theodora, sit down and hush, girl. They about to send *you* to the Wellness Center, acting like that."

I choked on my water, and the three of us erupted into giggles as Theodora took a seat.

"Out! Now!" The librarian said, stomping toward us. She was a short, round woman with moles all over her face that looked like chocolate chips.

"We didn't even get a warning? Just kicked out?" Theodora challenged. She stood in front of the librarian and towered over her—all six feet of her.

"Nooww!" the woman repeated, and other people turned around to look at us.

"It's not that serious, Theodora. Let's just go!" Naomi packed her bags and cleared her table.

"But we didn't even do anything!" Theodora fussed and grabbed her things.

She was definitely feeling herself these days after her big track championship win. Track and Field was Titus University's moneymaker, and Theodora was damn near a celebrity these days. If she thought she was about to take on a librarian; we needed a front-row seat.

"Let's just go, Theo. It's not a big deal." I backed away to the door. "I have to get to Synergy House, anyway." I lied. Work wasn't for another two hours.

"Fine!" Theodora huffed. She eyed the librarian once more, who was gazing up at Theodora throwing her shade. This was a different side of Theodora today, and Naomi and I peered at each other trying to figure out who or what we were seeing.

The three of us left the library, or maybe thrown out was a better way to explain what just happened in five minutes.

"I can't believe she made us leave! That cow!"

"You didn't have to challenge her like that." Naomi zipped her jacket and squinted at Theodora. "It was still funny as hell, though." She choked back a laugh. Before long, we were holding our stomachs and giggling again.

These girls were crazy. We all were in some way, I guess.

Two hours later, I arrived at Synergy House, and I was starving. I gave mom another fifteen dollars so she could get something for lunch, and that left nothing for me. My stomach growled as I searched around in Harper's office fridge for something to munch on before we started our meeting.

"You can have some of that banana pudding in there." Harper breezed in. And I mean, breezed; her floor-length kimono winded behind her.

"Who made it?"

"Kyle's wife. One of the copywriters on the eighth floor," she said, taking off her kimono.

I grabbed a spoon, took a large scoop, and shoved it into my mouth. The sweet custard hit all of my tastebuds and my eyes lit up. "This is so good!" I smacked my lips and licked the spoon.

"What's so good?" Tristan asked, walking into Harper's office.

"This banana pudding. Try some." I pushed a plastic spoon his way.

"Dude, I am not eating that stuff. I have to make weight for wrestling." He pushed the spoon away.

"What is that smell?" Bryce asked. His face was turned up, and he covered his nose as he walked in with a folder full of papers.

"Banana pudding. Want some?" I stuck out the spoon.

"I'm allergic to bananas. I told you guys that before!" Bryce pushed the spoon away from him.

"That's right! You did say that, Bryce. I think I should get some demographic information about you guys or something. You know emergency contacts, allergies. Epi-pen info. Things like that in case something happens. They mentioned in our supervisors' meetings a few months ago that the HR forms were missing, but it slipped my mind." Harper giggled. "I'll have a form or something made up." She scribbled on a Post-It note on her desk.

Kathleen walked in as I was licking the rim of the jar. She stopped and stared at me as my cheeks reddened.

"Thanks for meeting team. We have our first official over-night team-building seminar set! In three weeks,' time, we will spend the night in the Driskill Mountains getting to know each other and learning to co-exist as part of a team. I know I need some help in that department, as a supervisor." Harper snorted.

Bryce did too.

"Anyway. Clear your schedules for that day! Here is a ten-tative schedule I created and also a bagged lunch form from the dining hall. Please circle your food options so we can have something delicious to eat made fresh by the culinary team!"

Harper handed out paperwork and consent forms for us to sign. I wondered where I would be in three weeks' time. Would Mom still be around? I pulled my phone from my pocket and saw no missed calls from her. Or from Sidney. Or from King.

"Next things next! I reviewed everyone's articles that were submitted. Good work everyone! I especially liked Bryce's exposé about Mr. Chestnut. Such a shame that they still haven't found him, and to think, his poor wife was being abused that whole time and chose not to tell anyone. I didn't know that part until I read Bryce's article. Just goes to show, you never know someone behind closed doors." Harper shook her head. "And Indy. Your article about the Wellness Center was also enlightening and a fresh take on what needs to be improved on campus. A few editing errors, but otherwise it's good to go. We'll still lead with that one on the front page." Harper wrote our names on the dry erase board.

"Wait a minute. I write about a missing coach, and she gets to make the front page? How does that work?"

Harper spun around and tightened her lips. "Mr. Fuller, I have decided where each article should go, and that is my decision. Thank you for your concerns," she said, and turned back around at the board. Whenever Harper was irritated with Bryce, he turned into Mr. Fuller.

Bryce sat back down and shot a glare at me. I had nothing to do with Harper's decision to place which article where, and frankly, I didn't care. I had just wrote the thing hours earlier in the library with my friends. It was hard enough putting those words down on paper and being okay with them being read out loud. Per Theodora and Naomi, I was doing it anyway. Shit, if I hadn't killed Mr. Chestnut myself, I would say his article about his disappearance was a bigger story than the Wellness Center, too, but who was I?

"I'm out of here. I've had enough of this favoritism." Bryce grabbed his bag and shuffled out of the room. Kathleen, Tristan, and I peered around at each other, dumbfounded.

"And that, ladies and gentlemen, is how you get moved to the horoscopes section of a newspaper!" Harper rolled her eyes and sighed.

I pulled my phone and texted Theodora with quick fingers.

ME: Wait 'til I tell you about your boy, later!

CHAPTER THIRTEEN

MOM HAD POPCORN all over The Bus, and I cringed, thinking about Chaquille vacuuming the car. His favorite thing to do on the weekends was shine up and clean the interior, and he would have a field day with all the kernels littering the floor.

"And so I told him, 'Dad, you can't challenge the Tunica Rivers Police to a canoeing race.'" Mom chuckled. When she laughed, tears ran down her face and she didn't wipe or try to hide them. She grinned through the wetness staining her cheeks. "He had said, *'those simps can't beat me, I sent it in my dreams!'*" She slapped her hands on the dashboard.

Back in the day, Grandpa Ez challenged the water patrol units to an old-fashioned rowing race for no real reason at all. He always thought he was above the law, and he talked to them the same way he talked to my dad—with a hint of contempt. With my dad, it seemed more out of love, but with the police, well, what did that seem to be? I couldn't ask him anymore. I couldn't ask him anything anymore. I stared off into space. Had the police really killed my grandfather? While the world

continued on like it didn't happen? But it happened. It did. I laid my head against the seat and picked at my nails.

"Ez. . . Good ol' Ez." I sighed.

Mom stopped talking and popcorn shot out of her mouth. She threw kernels out the window to the ducks. "This is why it's even more important to do this, Indy. They have to pay. The police department killed my father, and your grandfather. It's time for two Rippers to take out the Jacks! And Sidney. We have to get Sidney."

"I know. I know," I said, hiding behind sniffles that wouldn't stop coming. "Get Sidney how?"

"We have to get her on our side, Indy Lindy. We have to get her with the ladies. I had me a thought." Mom's eyes glistened. "We go sit out front of the police station and we have an old-fashioned stake out. We wait for one of them to come out and boom! Kidnap one of them and then?" Mom's eyebrows jumped as she stared at me for confirmation.

"And then, what?"

"Whatever you have in mind, my girl?" She grinned with a corn kernel stuck to one of her teeth.

"I don't know, Mom. I just don't think kidnapping a police officer is a smart thing to do. Is it even really kidnapping?" I asked incredulously. I fought to be here, and even Harper stuck her neck out on the line for me. I needed to prove that I was worthy of being here. To whom, I didn't know. Maybe it was to me.

"Oh, don't be cute!" Mom squinted her eyes at me. "Do you have anything better, Sherlock Holmes?"

Mom and I snickered at her comment and the rest of her popcorn fell from the bag onto the floor, which made us laugh even harder.

I looked out over the inlet and surveyed the area, hoping no one saw us as I wiped the funny tears from my eyes. When my mom was around, I had a lot of those funny tears. She asked me to take her to the water, where her mom and dad used to take her and she could listen out for them. *Listen out for them*, she said. I was always listening out for them. And waiting and watching. I took her to the same place where I had spread Ez's ashes, and I couldn't help but look around to make sure we weren't being tailed or spotted. We were dangerously close to Tunica Rivers and although I was itching to go home and see Paisley and convince Sidney once more not to leave us; I dared not bring Mom into Tunica Rivers. We would for sure be hunted down, taken back to Trochesse, and if they found out my crimes, cart me off with her.

I wondered what type of person Mom would be back in Tunica Rivers. Would the memories from a lifetime ago come rushing back to her in tidal waves? Or would she not miss a beat and keep on keeping on like a penny skipping through the water? Even though I wanted to know my mom without restrictions or rules in place, I couldn't take her to the one place I knew I'd get to see that side of her.

Home.

"No, I don't have anything better right now, Mom. But we can't just sit outside the police station and wait for someone to come out. We need a better plan than that." I rolled up my window and swatted away a mosquito.

Mom was quiet for a few minutes before she slapped my knee. "You're right, my dear daughter." Her English voice had returned. "Until next time. Let's reconvene when we have a sound plan, my love. Break!" She nodded her head.

"Break!" I chuckled. My cell phone rang, interrupting our team meeting with an unknown number flashing across my screen.

"Hello?" I raised my hands to my lips to shush Mom.

She sucked her teeth.

"Hi, Ms. Indigo? This is Laylah Capri."

"Hi Laylah!" I sat up straight in the car. Being a member of the *Black Feminist Nation* came with some really cool t-shirts and powerful meetings with the influencer and hood feminist herself, Laylah Capri. But truth be told, I would do it for nothing. Laylah's compelling words spoke to me in a way that told me I needed a notebook every time I was around her. I wanted to write everything she said so I wouldn't forget a thing. I wanted to come back from her speeches and try out her same monologue in the mirror. Was I that dynamic? Could I be? I wondered why Laylah was calling me today. Our next meeting wasn't for another two weeks.

"Hey Indy! I don't mean to bother you after-hours, I have a request. I read your article about *The Wellness Center* and grief. They were so well put together; I was hoping you could use your platform to write something about the *Black Feminist Nation*? Nothing big, but since we have our Founder's Ball at the end of the semester, I thought we could seize the opportunity for more donors to sponsor our events next year."

"I'm honored, Laylah." I beamed. My heart swelled with pride, real, real wide.

"Wow! Thanks, Indy! This will be so good for BFN. I'll send over the details later."

I spit out my email address and hung up, dumfounded and awestruck.

"Laylah Capri wants me to write an article!" My eyes darted around and my breathing quickened.

"And who is this woman?" Mom looked confused.

"Remember I told you our newspaper came out this week? I left a copy for you to read. She's an activist on campus. I'm in her organization. Mom, this is major. . . for me . . ." I sucked in a sharp breath.

"My girl. Nothing is *not* major for you; not with your many gifts. You get that from your Mama Jackie. Go'on shine in the light, girl." Mom tapped my leg. This time, she wiped tears from her eyes.

CHAPTER FOURTEEN

"**Y**OU KNOW, I went to an all-white high school. It wasn't bad. I know many people try to paint a story of minorities being bullied all the time and outrageous racism that was visible in every way. I never experienced those things. They didn't call me the N word or anything like that. I thought I had it good, in a lot of ways. I thought I was lucky to go to such a school, because I knew what the alternative was down the street at those other schools where a lot of the Black kids went. They called those charter schools, and they had metal detectors and security guards out front."

Laylah Capri sat on the table and her legs swung back and forth. She wore a long-sleeved sweater, which said **Built Not Broken by B. Phillips**, and her mane was cut short, buzzed in the back with dirty blond ends. We both rocked short hair, only she looked like a movie star, while I looked like a little drummer boy.

I pulled my bucket hat down harder over my head as she continued talking.

"After my four years was up, I realized something. Even though I didn't have the militarized version of school, my time there could have been the same experience as those other students at the school down the street. Why? Because I dared to look past my own skin color and gender and educate myself more than my Vanilla counterparts. While they freely offered other students scholarships, I had to go into the offices and request them. When it came time to take the SATs, my counselor called me down to the office and gave me a hardship waiver that I didn't ask for. I didn't notice these things. I was high off life and excited to take on the world like most teenagers. Now that I am older, I want us to change the conversation. I want us to use our talents, and our skills, and everything else we can bring to the table and together. Let's build the table, Ladies. We are the *Black Feminist Nation*, which is a double whammy these days. You can be Black, but a feminist too. They probably think we're a bunch of hard-pressed lesbians."

I giggled and covered my mouth. The other girls in the room were also chuckling and watching Laylah Capri with wondrous eyes.

"Now we have quite a few events coming up, and I believe everyone has their assignments. Let's make the biggest impact we can on this campus and help ensure that education is fair and equitable. Go be great, ladies."

Laylah nodded in our direction, and it was like she saw me. She really saw me. I scribbled down notes for my article feverishly, so I didn't miss a thing. If she wanted something written to showcase BFN, then I was her girl. I would write an article so good that Harper would have no other choice but to put it on the front page again and call attention to the subtle inequities that existed. I wondered how my life would have turned out if I had a Laylah Capri when I was in high school? Maybe someone like her would've talked me off the ledge when Jaxon came at me. Maybe I wouldn't have pushed

him down the stairs and stuffed him in the incinerator. That was water under the bridge now, though, just like Mr. Chestnut was water under the bridge. I couldn't take it back, but it made me wonder if I was a product of my environment like so many other students.

Damn, I wish Mom was here to see this. She was all about girl power and sticking it to the man. I never noticed it before, but as I gazed around at all different shades of brown, feminine faces. Had we all experienced the same indirect slights? The same insinuations? I thought I was alone in my feelings, but it never occurred to me that other people had similar struggles. I mean, I'm sure their struggles didn't end in murder three times over, but still. They had them.

I squeezed through the crowd and made my way toward Laylah.

When she saw me, she broke into a big smile. "Hey there. How's the article coming along?"

"Pretty good. I think I have some great material!" I beamed. "It should be ready for the print run next week."

"Sounds good, thank you for helping the cause." Laylah grabbed my shoulders and pulled me into a long embrace. Laylah smelled like a sweater fresh out of the dryer, and I wanted to inhale her. I wanted to be—her.

Even though it was already late, I rushed to Synergy House to write. The words seemed to pour out of me. When I got there, everyone was gone for the evening except for Bryce, who was typing away at his computer. I rolled my eyes. I was hoping to have the place to myself before me and Chaquille headed to Tunica Rivers for the weekend. But here was this crud dud.

"What are you doing here so late?" I slammed my bag down on the table and took off my jacket.

"Figured I would get some work done on this article before it's due on Monday."

"Any updates with the Chestnut story?" I pensively asked, while logging into my computer. Saying the name out loud excited me and made me nervous all at the same time.

"Not really. It seemed like a good idea, but the police have no more information, it seems... It's like he disappeared into thin air. I really don't know how more people aren't up in arms about this." Bryce sighed and tapped at his computer.

"Maybe you should write about something else, then," I suggested.

"Good work Indy, throw him off the scent!" a voice in my head screamed.

I sat up straight. It had been weeks since I had heard the voices, and when the voices came, so did some drama I couldn't turn down.

"Why would I do that?" Bryce frowned. "This is a good story. It just needs more meat and potatoes. What is it you're writing about, anyway? I'm sure you'll make the front page, per usual." He sulked into his chair.

I told no one besides Mom about my article with the *Black Feminist Nation.* I wanted it to be private, something I crafted myself with no direction from Harper or input from the team. Bryce couldn't say it was nepotism this time. I wanted to present the article at our next meeting to shocked faces—Bryce included.

"I'm just getting some ideas together for something I want to write in the future." I lied. He didn't need to know anything that I was doing. I wrote and wrote for the next hour and a half. My fingers danced around the keyboard as I put words and feelings to my thoughts about Laylah, her mission for the BFN, and what it meant to me to be a part of it. I also wrote about my own experiences at Tunica Rivers High School, and angry tears sprang to my eyes as I remembered Jaxon's friend breaking my camera that I went to painstaking lengths to

borrow from the library. Racism was subtle, all right. Until it wasn't.

I put the finishing touches on my article and pressed save. Warm feelings washed over me as I nodded my head in approval at myself. This article was good. I felt it. I glanced over the monitor at Bryce slumped back in his chair with a surly look on his face. He had barely typed since I got there. I was about to sign out of the computer and ask him if he was okay when my phone rang.

"Hello?" I answered.

"What time are you coming back? I want to go to Walmart before you go back to Tunica." Mom asked.

"I'm just finishing up here," I said, grabbing my jacket and bag. Time got away from me and I was running late. "Are you going to be here late?" I whispered to Bryce.

He ran his fingers through his hair and scrunched his eyebrows. "Yeah, I'll be here for a while. I have to get this article done." For a second, and I mean a second, I felt bad for Bryce. He worked this Chestnut angle as hard as he could but thankfully for me, it wasn't working out.

"Well, I'm heading out." I rushed and grab my things. "I'm leaving this weekend out of town."

"Have fun. I'll be right here," he said with a grunt.

"Do you think it looks cheap?" Dad asked.

Chaquille and I peered around at the living room area where Dad ripped back the carpeted floors to expose the hardwood. They were in terrible shape, not that I knew much about hardwood floors anyway, but if this is what they were supposed to look like, we were in for some trouble.

"Ummm." Chaquille started. He bit his lip before he spoke. "They don't look bad, Mr. Barre. But they don't look good either."

Dad sighed and looked around. Renovating a house for tenants was more work than he expected. Coupled with all the rules and regulations that the city imposed, Dad was a one-man band working around the clock trying to get it up to par.

"I thought the houses would be ready by early next year, but with so much work still to be done, I'm just not sure we'll have it ready by that time."

"Dad, don't worry. We'll get it together. That's why we're here, to help as much as we can. And we still have the other house by Titus' campus and the one back in Tunica that are almost ready to go. It'll be fine."

"Things shouldn't look slapped together. I didn't get the most expensive materials, and I didn't go for the brand-new hardwoods or brand-new counters. I'm trying to save as much money as I can, but also make this place livable for someone else. This is our future, Indy. Your future. I stepped down from the retirement home for this. And one day, it will be all yours." He swung his hands around the house.

I didn't have the heart to tell him I didn't see myself being a landlord, nor did I see myself living in Tunica Rivers. I didn't know where I was supposed to be yet, but Tunica Rivers haunted me something terrible. Sidney wouldn't say, but I think she felt the same. I didn't blame her for wanting to leave us.

I wondered if he had heard from Mom, but I'm sure that he hadn't. He would have told me and he would've made the long trek to Titus University to confront me in person himself if he knew—that I knew—that Mom was here. I couldn't bring it up right now, not with Chaquille here *and* this being his first official visit to Tunica Rivers. I left Mom back in Titus, where she said she had made some friends.

"Let's just work in the living room today and tomorrow we'll start in the bathrooms. Those are in the worst shape," Dad said. He looked around bewildered like he was afraid that he had taken on too much, too soon.

Before I could interject, Chaquille said, "Mr. Barre, that's why we're here to help this weekend. The properties closest to Titus, Indy and I will be responsible for. You can take care of the one in Tunica Rivers. Okay?" He nodded in Dad's direction.

Dad was a short and chubby man and Chaquille towered over him. He looked down at my dad and extended his hand. Dad looked up at Chaquille for what seemed like a long time, he reached out, and shook his hand back. I slipped on shoe protectors over my sneakers, so they didn't get messed up from the exposed floors, took off my bracelets, and set them in my bag. I got ready to help Dad, help us, help the family.

CHAPTER FIFTEEN

"INDY! HOW'VE YOU been?" Tyson looked me up and down.

I pushed the cart holding laminate hardwood floors to Dad's pick-up truck, while Chaquille hopped out of the front seat to meet me at the flatbed in front of the hardware store.

"Tyson? Oh my goodness, it's been years!" I smiled. Tyson was the son of my former boss at Dennis and Son's Funeral Home. Mr. Dennis gave me my first grown-up job as a funeral attendant and he performed Ez's funeral service for a steep discount. I would forever be grateful.

"What are you doing here? I thought you were some big-time college girl now? At least, that's how my dad describes you." He chuckled.

Tyson's lanky frame smelled of weed, and his eyes were glassy. Typical Tyson. Some things never changed.

"My dad bought a few houses to rent out so we're helping him renovate. This is my boyfriend, Chaquille." I motioned, as Chaquille and Tyson shook hands.

"That's so cool. Let me help you guys get this stuff loaded," Tyson offered.

"Be my guest."

I stood back and let the men do the heavy lifting. Chaquille and I spent the night before helping Dad lay more flooring. After three hours of arguing and checking YouTube videos for tutorials, we finally gave up and called it a night. We were back at it today; me with a sore back and Chaquille complaining of shoulder pain.

"You know, Indy. My dad is thinking about selling the place. You should stop by and see him sometime."

"Sell the place! He loves that funeral home! Why is he thinking of selling?" I gasped.

Tyson scratched his head and shrugged. "Beats me. I always thought he loved that place more than he did me, but since Mom passed, he just doesn't have the same spark for it."

I swallowed. Tyson was talking about his dad, but he was speaking to my life. With Ez gone, I wasn't sure I had the same spark for anything either. I found it sometimes in my writing, and even with Chaquille. But there were other times when I was sitting in class, and I would drift off to a place that smelled like pine trees beyond Ez's house. I would spend time with Theodora and Naomi and I would feel guilty for laughing and having a good time.

Guilt tasted so sour sometimes. Like when you poured yourself a bowl of cereal, not knowing the milk was bad. You take a giant spoonful to your mouth and spit it out and cringe. Guilt tasted the same way, only I couldn't get the taste out of my mouth.

"I will stop by and see him. Is he there now?"

Tyson chuckled. "Of course, he is. He's always there. Every morning by 7 A.M., ain't nothing changed."

He wasn't there the morning I killed Jaxon. A smile crept to my face.

Chaquille and I said our goodbyes to Tyson. Instead of going to meet Dad at the property, I hung a left onto Humbert St and took it straight down until Dennis and Son's Funeral Home entered my sights.

"So this is where you used to work. It's creepy." Chaquille eyed the place as I parked out front.

"Do you want me to come in?" He fumbled with his seatbelt, ready to unbuckle himself.

I placed my hand over his. "No, I won't be long. You can stay here and watch the stuff in the back." I leaned over and kissed his lips. "And put some Chapstick or something on. Those things feel like Brillo pads."

Chaquille glared at me and grabbed my shirt into a fist and pulled me toward him. "You love me anyway, woman. Crusty lips and all!"

I fixed my shirt as I walked to the front of Dennis and Son's. I smoothed the little bit of hair that I had, and I pulled at the bottom of my t-shirt. My heart was beating as I hit the buzzer.

"Greetings, dear visitor. How may I be of assistance?" Mr. Dennis' voice echoed out of the speaker.

Relief washed over me. He was still the same quirky person. It was me who was different.

In a few minutes, Mr. Dennis buzzed me inside and scooped me up into his arms in a bear hug.

"Indy Lindy! My Indy is back like she never left. Let me look at you! You done went and chopped off all your hair like that Britney Spears girl? Are you okay? How's your daddy? I heard he's buying up all the properties around town! I'm still so sorry about your Grandpa Ez. Actually, your mama too. They still ain't found her, huh? Don't worry, your dad told me she was on the lam." Mr. Dennis winked and shot out questions at rapid speed. I answered none of them as I took in the sights and sounds of the place where my first kill took place.

"She's back!"

"I knew she would come see us!"

"Hip, hip, hooray!"

"Indigo is coming to towwwwwnn."

The voices came fast and I blinked, holding onto the wall to steady myself. My breathing was heavy, and I felt faint. The smell of embalming fluid was so strong, and it was a scent that I would never forget. It enveloped me in a fog.

"You okay, girl?" Mr. Dennis held my arm as I fell into him.

"I'm okay." I breathed. "You've made a lot of changes to the place."

I looked around. Mr. Dennis put in new LED lights and replaced the old, dingy carpets with new clean, tile. The same old-school drapes hung, a chalky brown color that probably had been hanging there for the past twenty years. It looked and smelled like the same place I remembered, only brighter and cleaner.

Mr. Dennis saw me checking out the place. "You like the changes?" Before I could respond, he kept right on talking. "I'm glad you're here to see it for yourself." He gave a smug nod. "Tyson doesn't care one way or the other. I knew you would appreciate it, though."

What made him think I would appreciate it? I didn't particularly enjoy working at the funeral home. It was the place that housed my greatest shame. Even with the voices conversing throughout the place, tearing through my every thought, there was a stillness here that brought me solace.

I said nothing to Mr. Dennis as I gazed around.

"Let's walk." He held a hand to my back and led me through the space. "I had quite a few things updated. I'm thinking of selling the place."

"Why is that?" My voice was barely above a whisper and the voices screamed over me.

"Are you here to help him?"

"Can you reach out to my family? I want to be cremated, not buried!"

"Does anyone know what in the world I'm doing here?"

The voices were rampant.

Mr. Dennis's too big business suit hung off him and I noticed he lost some weight. He rocked his fedora hat cocked off the side, and he tucked a feather in its place. "I just think it's time. I've put my life into this place, and maybe it's time I go off and buy me a boat, or something. Move to Florida."

"A boat? Florida? What's in Florida?" I sat down on a bench in the foyer.

"You know all us old folks retire to Florida." Mr. Dennis's shoulders jiggled while he chuckled.

"Actually, let me show you Shelby! We got her a new motor, and she's been kicking at top speed!"

I clutched the wall as splotches of black interrupted my vision. "Shelby?"

"You remember Shelby, now! It ain't been that long!"

Mr. Dennis pulled my arms and tugged me to my feet, pushing the double doors open into a small room in which Shelby sat. I remembered Shelby all too well; it was where Jaxon met his demise.

I studied the incinerator as a sea of voices shouted back at me. There were so many of them; I couldn't make out what they were saying. One voice I heard loud and clear.

Jaxon.

"Wow, Indy. Was it really that serious?" he murmured.

"Indigo. Not, Indy," I said out loud. My voice cracked hearing him and I felt nervous.

"What was that?" Mr. Dennis shot me a confused face.

"Nothing, I said Shelby looks good." I lied.

Mr. Dennis beamed. "I thought so too. You know, Indy. If you are interested, you can take on this place. I trust you and your daddy. He is a hardworking man, and so are you. If you would like to run it while I'm in Florida, as you young kids

say it; living my best life—you can take over Dennis and Son's. I guess then we can call it Dennis and Daughter's."

I looked at Mr. Dennis and leaned against Shelby. The voices were too much to bear. Could I run this place? Did I even want to? The answer came to me easily, and I didn't need any voices to help.

I didn't want to live in Tunica Rivers.

Living far away from here and even further away from the voices was the goal. Dennis and Son's was my first big-girl job, and I was grateful to Mr. Dennis for trusting me with his most prized possession, but this place would be the death of me if I stayed. I needed to finish college, and to make sure I could come back to Tunica Rivers when I *wanted* to, not when because I *had* to.

"No, thank you Mr. Dennis. I really appreciate that offer, but I want to finish college first and explore my options," I said, placing a hand on the side of Shelby.

"Aww, no problem, girl. If you change your mind, let me know. This place will always be home to me, and I like to think it holds a special place for you, too."

A special place. Indeed, it was. Indeed, it was.

A few minutes later, I was holding my breath and sitting in my car. Even though it was the morning, the Dennis and Son's neon sign lit up like the secrets it held couldn't be contained any longer. Chaquille's anger emanated from his passenger seat.

My phone rang and it was Minko Forrest.

"Your mom has been spotted in Quakerville. It's about 15 miles from Titus University, so I think she is making her way towards you. Indigo. Please reach out if she accosts or is aggressive in any way."

"Aggressive? She's not aggressive."

With a point-blank tone, he said, "Ms. Indigo, a jury decided that years ago, not me."

My hand squeezed my cellphone.

"We only have a few more days until the state will announce it to the public."

"Why haven't they already?"

"Well, these things are complicated. Or at least they like us to believe. From what I know, it's an election year and the governor doesn't want to scare the public with news of an asylum escapee. Especially one who killed a war veteran. You know how those *Thin Blue Line* folks can be. I guess that's just too much like right," he said.

My eyes softened and my tongue released from the roof of my mouth. Once again, I liked Mr. Minko Forrest. He was a straight shooter, and I knew what to expect.

"Okay, I understand."

"Good. I hope to speak to you soon, Ms. Indigo. Stay safe out there."

Chaquille cocked his head and peered at me with one eye. "Your mom escaped? When did this happen?"

"A few weeks ago."

"And you didn't think to tell me?"

I said nothing. Rays from the sign flickered.

"Indigo. Your mom has escaped from that. . . that. . . place she lives in. From killing a man. And you.didn't.tell.me?" he said, enunciating every syllable on every word.

"See! There it is! There it is!" I banged my hand on the steering wheel.

"What!" Chaquille screamed back.

"Judgement. You're judging my mom… my family… me …"

"Indigo. I'm not judging you. But when will you let someone in? You have this fucked up way of waiting until the last possible

moment to drop bombs. I could be there for you, you know? The way you were there for me." Chaquille's voice cracked.

I choked back tears threatening to drop down my cheeks. I didn't want to cry in front of him.

But why, Indy. Why? a voice in me whispered.

And I couldn't tell if it was my own voice or one of the real voices. They were real to me at least.

"I don't know!" I whimpered. And I didn't know. I really didn't. The only person I had really let in these days was Trenita, and I hardly saw her anymore. I had people that I spent time with like Theodora and Naomi. But I never let them *in*.

"Let me be here for you. Indy. I love you."

Just as Chaquille spoke his last syllable, the neon sign clicked off for the night, and the skies opened up with soft rain.

"Let me be there for you," Chaquille whispered and kissed my forehead. Rained tapped at my window, and a tear slipped down my cheek.

CHAPTER SIXTEEN

"**S**HE LOOKS LIKE your dad." Chaquille grinned at Paisley.

"Doesn't she? I said she's going to grow up and look like one of those girls who look just like they daddy in pigtails and a dress!" Ms. Arletha cooed over Chaquille's shoulder.

Dad's hands were white and soapy as he twirled one of those swishy cleaner things in Paisley's bottle. He wiped his hands, paddled into the living room in his man flops, and put his arms over Ms. Arletha's shoulders. "Ain't nothing wrong with looking like her daddy," he fussed. "I don't see what the issue is."

Ms. Arletha shrieked and her hand whipped to her mouth, stifling a giggle at Dad's expense. "Benjamin, my child may look like you, but she will not have feet smelling like yours! I'm so happy you got the houses now. Your work boots from the retirement home were enough to make me question everything!"

Before Dad purchased the houses to renovate, he worked ten-to-fifteen-hour shifts at the retirement home and dedicated every waking moment to being at their beck and call. I remembered grumbling about how much time he spent

away from home, even though I knew it was all for us. Dad was older now and Paisley needed his presence even more than the retirement home would allow. Dad worked so hard to make sure he had money to pay for the things we needed when the whole time the things we needed were free. This. Right here. And it didn't cost a thing. The houses really could be our ticket out. To a life full of ease. I looked around at my family and Chaquille. I could see my dad's vision so clear.

I grinded my teeth and thought about Sidney. Everything my dad was trying to do included her, too. Stomping down the hallway, I flung the door open. "Are you going to come and spend time with us and Paisley?"

She looked up at me with wide, empty eyes; laying on her stomach with her journal sprawled in front of her and different color gel pens. "No, I'm okay. I saw her earlier. You can see her." She gave a weak smile.

I had had enough.

"Sidney. You are not going to live with your dad. I know things are. . . hard right now, with Ez." I stepped into her room and closed the door. Her bed creaked under my weight, and I crouched next to her. The words were caught in my throat, but so was a knot of fear that I would lose Sidney too. I couldn't lose her too. She wasn't the same shy little girl that grabbed her grandfather around the neck and begged for horseback rides. She was a girl already going through the throes of teenage-hood and grief. She was grieving, too.

Sidney hurried to close her journal. "Indy, I don't want to hear it."

"Well, you're going to hear it." My voice raised. "It wasn't just you who lost Ez! We all did. You were close to him, but so was I! He'll never get to meet Paisley. . . and. . . we need you here. We're a team and if one is missing from the dozen, then it's not a dozen anymore." The words spilled out of me until I was

almost shouting. My hands gripped the sides of Sidney's bed, and I balled my fists while yelling everything I was thinking for the past few weeks. I yelled and tears flowed. She wasn't allowed to leave us. I was the one dealing with voices. The murders. The one hiding Mom in my dorm room.

Even so, I hoped she was okay while I shouted at Sidney. "You know I've been calling your dad. To talk about this. He still hasn't gotten back to me."

Sidney shrugged. "He said that you called. He's working on some big project for the record label that's got his full attention right now."

"Sidney, please. Don't do this." I kneeled in front of my sister. I so needed her. I still had so many questions about King, his conversation with mom, or his plans for Sidney. No official moves were made quite yet, but there was a court date in about a month to discuss custody in front of a judge. The entire reason Sidney moved in with us was because King didn't have time to fully care for her, and now he didn't have time to even respond to my phone call. What type of father was he? Benjamin Barre would never. *Had* never.

"Indy. Everything alright?" Dad asked. Ms. Arletha's shoulder touched his as she rocked Paisley in her arms in the hallway. Chaquille was next to her, peeking his head around the corner. I could tell by his steps he was unsure. Nervous. Unaware of his place in this family drama that unfolded in front of him. I told him more about my family last night in the car than I told anyone. I didn't tell him about the voices or the part where Mom was holed up in my dorm room. Not that part.

"No, everything is not okay. Sidney is *not* going to live with her dad. I said what I said." I glared at Sidney, but I wasn't angry. I was hurt. Confused. Shocked. How could she? How?

"I think that is her decision to make, Indy Lindy. We don't want her to go, and Paisley needs her big sister here. But it is

her decision. We'll find out more in a few weeks at the court hearing," Ms. Arletha uttered. Paisley squirmed and fussed, and I wondered if she knew there was some funky energy around here. That I was the funky energy.

"And what do you think?" I glared at Dad not saying a word. He was always quiet when it seemed to matter.

"Indy Lindy. 'Letha is right, baby. It is her decision."

"Ahhh you guys aren't hearing me!" I screamed, and a shout escaped my lungs that I hadn't heard since I lifted Jaxon's ass and hoisted him into Shelby the Incinerator. Why were they giving her options? Weren't they the grownups and didn't grownups decide? If I was fourteen and told my dad I was moving out, he would laugh in my face. But the circumstances were different. So different and Dad wasn't really her dad, and King *was* her dad, but as much as he was absent, he wasn't her dad *either*. It was all so confusing. When I peered down at Sidney's teary-eyed face, I saw myself. A sad girl, singing the hearts blues and missing Ez.

"And what about Mom? No one is thinking of her in this situation! What will she think of this?"

"Indy-Lindy, they still haven't found your mom, and honestly, I don't think she is even a factor in this equation."

"She's always a factor!" I seethed. Minko Forrest had called Dad too so he knew she was out there somewhere.

"They're trying to gang up on Indy! Oh, we're not doing this!" The voices in my head screamed.

"Indy, calm down. It's okay." Chaquille stepped forward and patted my shoulder.

"It's not okay! We are a family and we all have sacrificed. We all lost Ez! Not just Sidney. I can't lose her too. I just can't." I sobbed into Chaquille's arm, wetting his shirt.

Chaquille sat down next to me on Sidney's bed and held me as I whimpered.

"I'm gonna go put Paisley down ya'll." Ms. Arletha backed out of the room.

"Indy. You can't decide for her. It's her choice. I don't want Sidney to go either, but this is hard for her and she's made her decision."

"Indy. Please don't be mad at me." Sidney held a pillow to her chest as tears streamed down her face.

Her bed moaned and groaned under the weight of me, Sidney, and Chaquille. It sounded like I felt. Chaquille's presence calmed me and soon, my whimpers quieted. He felt like chicken soup to my soul, but my soul was also calling for something else that I couldn't deny. Another presence that calmed me. Another chicken soup, but this one I hadn't tasted in a while.

I stood up and pushed past Dad and Chaquille.

"Indy, where are you going!" Chaquille shouted.

He was hot on my heels, but I knew the corners of this house better than he did. Taking a sharp left turn, I ducked into the living room and grabbed my keys to The Bus off the table and slid out the back door. I fired up The Bus, scenes of my outburst fresh in my mind. I didn't want Sidney to leave. Why did they act like it was okay? I wanted things back to normal and that included Ez and Mom back full time. I wanted Sidney to experience her, too. Screeching out of the driveway and barreling down the street, tears clouding my sight. I called Mom's cell phone over and over, but she didn't answer. My hand ached from gripping the phone too hard.

I took a sharp right and drove all the way down McTaugh Road. Making another right, and then another until a few miles passed me by and the houses were more spread out and their lawns manicured.

When I jerked into the driveway, the car lurched to a stop and I pulled the keys from the ignition. The front door flung open, and he walked out, frowning.

Will.

I stormed to the front door and when Will saw it was me through the opened glass door; he closed it until it was only a crack. His eyes were wide, but mine were crazed and wilder.

"Will! I'm sorry! I'm so sorry!" I cried. And I was sorry. *I was so sorry.* I never meant to hurt him.

Will's arm twitched, and he stared at me with equal parts of shock and excitement.

"This has gone on long enough. I'm not well. Not without you."

Will's eyes softened, but he didn't let his arm down. "Ain't nothing here for you, Indy. Go over there with what's-his-name?"

I scowled at the man I had shared my entire childhood with. "You know that's not true. And Ez. . . you know Ez isn't here. And now you're gone. Too. You're gone too." I hiccupped my way through my tears. Random sounds that sounded like words spilled from me and drool was on my lip, daring to drip. I was sure I looked like a crazy woman and I could see my short, boyish hair sticking up in all different directions in Will's foyer mirror behind him. "I miss you. I miss Will. I miss everyone I love." I cried. And cried and cried.

Will shifted his weight before he groaned. He hesitated before opening the door. He pulled me in and embraced me, placing flicks of light kisses across my face. I closed my swollen red eyes and they burned, man; they burned. It felt good to shut them and know I was safe, and he didn't hate me. My phone jingled in my pocket and I knew it was Dad or Chaquille, or even Mom looking for me. I collapsed under his smell, strength, and love needing to be held.

Will's parents stood behind Will and I. They shared a glance and Mr. Simms locked his fingers with Mrs. Simms and they smiled at each other—and then us.

CHAPTER SEVENTEEN

I STOOD BEHIND THEODORA and spotted her while she pumped iron. A dark vein popped out from her neck and I couldn't believe that I had allowed Naomi and Theodora to talk me into going to the gym today. Theodora's toned frame and chiseled muscles were something to look at, smooth and graceful. I was on a treadmill when Theodora asked me to spot her. *Spot her?* I only knew one thing about spotting, and that had nothing to do with pumping iron.

Naomi was across from us, sitting down on the mat with her legs stretched wide. She was taking selfies. Slinging a small towel over her shoulder, she tilted her head and made duck lips into her phone.

"Dig your heels in and be serious, Indy. You can't be lazy like that." Theodora huffed.

My eyes bugged out of my head. "Lazy? I didn't even want to come tonight, Flo Jo!"

Naomi giggled and normally, I would too, but I didn't like Theodora's tone.

Theodora let out a loud sulk and sat up from under the bar like I was being unreasonable.

"Now, now, simmer down, you two fire signs." Naomi waved her white towel.

Will was a fire sign. He was all fire, that one. Will and I spent a good five minutes tonguing each other down in the doorway of his house before his dad cleared his throat and said, *"Errr ahh, Indy. We're happy to see you. But can you come back at a decent hour?"*

I couldn't come back.

It was a long ride home back to Titus with Chaquille. I opted for the semi truth and told Chaquille that I went to Will's house. Chaquille was glued to his phone and acting funny ever since. Everything was an "uh-huh," and "okay."

"Anyway, Theodora, how is Dylan? I hardly see him anymore since we're not in the dorms." Naomi changed the subject.

Theodora's dark brown cheeks reddened, and she shied away. "He's good. We're good. We're so good." Theodora gushed. She nodded like she was convincing herself. She wasn't the type of girl to blush. Theodora always had a comeback for everything; but straight out of the Hamptons, boat-shoe wearing, Lacrosse loving Dylan made my best friend blush.

I scooted Theodora down as I sat beside her on the bench.

"And what about you? Anything new?"

"No, nothing over here." I shot out, apparently a little too quick because Naomi raised an eyebrow.

"And Sidney?" Naomi eyed me. I told the girls I went home for the weekend and my main goal was to talk to Sidney about this living with her dad business.

That went well.

Replaying the weekend in my mind took over like movie reels and before I knew it, I was telling them about Ez, Chaquille, Dad and his properties, Sidney, and Will. . . I told them about Will and every sorted detail of me descending on his doorstep like a crazed person. I even told them about Harper and her struggles with being a new supervisor.

"That reminds me. I'm going to help Bryce with his Mr. Chestnut story." Theodora smiled widely like she was doing a good deed.

What? She was helping *him*? "I didn't think there was anything to help with. Harper led with my story about the Wellness Center."

"Yeah, I know that. Your story was good, Indy. It was fantastic. But come on! Something happened here and I think it's worth checking out. What if he was murdered or something?"

"So what are you going to do, Sherlock Holmes?" My nostrils flared.

"I knew you would act like this." Theodora sucked her teeth. "Every time I bring up Mr. Chestnut, you get swole in the chest. Why, Indy?"

Naomi's eyes darted between me and Theodora, wondering what this exchange was we were having. I wondered too.

"I just don't think he was murdered or anything. I mean, I told you what type of person he was already. And no one believed me." I sneered.

"Is *that* what this is about? No one believed you and now you feel some type of way about it? That makes no sense, Indy." Theodora questioned. She picked up one of the fifteen-pound weights and began lifting with more intensity than before.

I stared at Theodora, my best friend. Was I wrong for trying to warn my friends about Mr. Chestnut? I wanted to keep them safe and free from any bullshit attached to him. But was that my job? My job was to be a student and make it through college, and that seemed to be the main job I let fall to the wayside.

An awkward silence fell between us. And it was Naomi who changed the subject. "Did you and Will . . ." She made a head nod and raised her eyebrows.

"No." I dropped my shoulders. "But I wanted to. I really wanted to."

"Indy." Theodora sighed, and I heard the disappointment in her voice. "What are you going to do? Are you going to tell Chaquille?"

"Tell him what?" My neck shot up and peered at her. "There's nothing to tell and we already discussed it." I lied. I didn't mention the kiss. I didn't always understand how I felt, and this was one of those moments.

"Oh, well, maybe you ran to your ex-boyfriend in your moment of need and left your current boyfriend at your parent's house. That's something." Theodora shrugged and rolled her eyes.

"Theodora! We don't need to ask those questions right now." Naomi slapped Theodora's leg with her hand towel. She pulled her legs together and sat criss-crossed. "Indy, how do you feel? Like really?"

I picked at a corner piece of the weight bench I was sitting on. I didn't know what to say and maybe that was a part of the problem. I was never saying what I felt. But if I told people some of the thoughts that were really in my mind, who would I still have in my corner? My mom was still in my room, waiting for my return, and I still couldn't tell anyone about that either. It was like, if I spoke my truth, I would lose the people I loved. But when the truth was stranger than fiction, and in this case, it was—was honesty still the best policy?

I swallowed. "Like a fraud. I feel like a fraud."

Theodora frowned.

I rushed back to my room to shower before I headed to work for a few hours. Mom was laying across my bed watching tv with Starburst wrappers littering the floor.

"Finally, girl. I thought you would never get back from that gym. I don't know how you young girls do it. I hate working out. A girl should only sweat doing one thing!"

"Ew, Mom." I peeled off my wet clothes and tossed them into the hamper in the closet. "Mom, that detective called. Someone spotted you; you have to be more careful!" I urged.

She blew right past my statement. "Anyway. I think I figured out a way for us to kidnap one of them cops from Tunica Rivers." She danced in place.

"Mom, we talked about this. I am not kidnapping a cop." I grumbled as I checked my phone. No texts from Will. Or Chaquille. Or King. I stopped by King's house with Chaquille before I left Tunica Rivers and Trent said he was on the road and that I should text him. Not call him, *text* him. What great parenting Sidney wanted to leave us for. Mom wore a large onesie we had picked up from the consignment shop and she wrapped her hair in a towel and a plastic bag while she deep conditioned her hair.

"Mom, make sure you don't get none of that oil on the bed," I pointed.

"Oh girl, don't worry, I've been doing this longer than you've been alive. Do you think you can get your hands on a white van?" she asked. She had a crazed look on her face and her head shook from side to side.

"Mom, where would I get a white van from?"

"I don't know, Indy. But you could be a bit more helpful here," she scoffed. "I'm coming up with all the solutions, and all you do is spend time with your boyfriend and your friends. And when are you going to let me meet this, Chaquille?"

I bit my lip. "I did tell him about you. Not about you being here, of course. But he knows you're not at Trochesse." Convincing Chaquille to spend our time in his own room these days instead of my own was easier than I thought it would be. As long as I was next to him, he didn't care where we slept. He trusted me, and I wasn't sure how I felt about that.

Mom hopped off the bed and oil slid down her neck and arms, seeping into my sheets. "Well bring that man over here! He got a daddy? Tell him to bring him too." Mom danced around my room. She hooted and grabbed my hips, shaking them from side to side. "Just quit this college thing girl, let's go on tour. I can teach you how to play the drums while I sing. The FatCats will be back like we never left." Mom gyrated her pelvis in front of me.

I giggled. "I'm running late and have to get to the office to write. Let's talk later." I grabbed my keys and stomped out of my room, which was becoming too small for the both of us.

Turning up the radio in The Bus, and letting Summer Walker take me to another place, I fumbled with the defroster control and banged my hand against the knobs as I tried to hit a happy median of defrosting the lightly chilled windows and keeping warm.

I grabbed my books and a water bottle from the backseat and made my way inside for the afternoon sessions. The place was unusually quiet, and I wondered if I was late for the meeting. No, I knew I wasn't. We held it every Thursday at 2 p.m. Harper said it was perfect siesta time; that bewitching 2 p.m. hour when my eyes got heavy.

Kathleen, Tristan, and Bryce huddled together in front of our computer stations, whispering.

I sat my bags down and hurried to the group. The hairs on the back of my arms stood. Something was wrong.

"What's going on?" I whispered. My hands were clammy.

"You haven't heard?" Kathleen asked, like she didn't just watch me walk in.

"Heard what?"

"Dude. Harper got fired. They are replacing her with some. . . some lame." Tristan filled in.

"Maybe now we'll get some real articles written around here. I don't see this as a problem. I mean, I complained about her." Bryce grinned. Kathleen and Tristan looked at him with disgust on their faces.

"Why would you do that?" Kathleen demanded an answer.

"Someone needed to do it. Seriously?" Bryce waved his hands.

I turned away from the group and called Harper's cell phone number; my hands trembling while the team argued behind me.

No answer.

I called her again. No answer.

"What's your problem?" I whipped around, facing Bryce.

"Whoa. Now I'm the bad guy. Come on! We all had issues with lunches, article distribution, things are chronically late. We STILL don't have access to the cloud server to back up our work even after asking a million times. It's bad for business and I don't know about the rest of you, but my career is depending on this, and I can't leave it to just some—"

"Some what? Some what?" I got in Bryce's face.

"Kill him, Indy!"

"Take him out!"

The voices bellowed in my head.

"Some. . . some . . weirdo." Bryce glowered.

"Dude. You are right. But you didn't have to go about it this way. Come on! This internship is important to me too,

you think you're the only one hesitant? You didn't have to do it this way though, bro. You really didn't." Tristan shook his head and frowned.

Kathleen, Tristan, and I shot looks at Bryce, and I wanted to smash his face in for fucking with Harper. She wasn't the best, but she meant well, and she was real. She was fam.

"Hello everyone. I am your new supervisor. My name is Robert John." A tall older white man breezed in and interrupted our skirmish. His hair was gelled to one side and his suit looked expensive and tight. "I would like to get our meeting started in about five minutes, so please print me out what you have been working on so we can start planning the next edition." Robert John gave a curt nod and turned back into his office, which used to be Harper's office.

The four of us shot eyes at each other, wondering if we should follow Robert John's lead. We didn't know a thing about him but what choice did we have?

Bryce's face was a deep shade of red. He sat down first and turned on his computer.

I exhaled the longest breath and tried not to pass out from the pain in my chest. I powered on the computer and noticed that the guest account and my personal account both said logged in.

That's weird.

I peered closer and frowned.

When I typed in my password, a bunch of Google pages popped open for pages that I hadn't been researching. This was definitely weird. I always closed everything out before I logged off. Or did I log off? My stomach lurched, and I clicked faster on the mouse, searching through my documents, but I didn't see it. I didn't see it anywhere.

My article about the *Black Feminist Nation* was gone. I never saved it to the computer Naomi gave me. When I wrote my

previous articles, I had to use a clunky flash drive that I kept losing, so for this one I decided to only write it on my Synergy House computer.

My eyes jumped around the screens, switching between pages. I even checked the recycle bin and searched every folder on the homepage. I didn't find it.

With no access to the cloud yet. It was gone. My article was gone.

CHAPTER EIGHTEEN

"**F**UCK!" I SCREAMED and pushed away from my computer.

"What's wrong?" Kathleen brushed over my shoulder, and her eyes roamed my screen in confusion.

"It's gone. My article is gone. Did the computers crash or something?" I balled my hands as I slammed them against the table. What in the actual fuck?

"Two minutes, everyone." Mr. John peeked his head out of his office and looked at his watch.

My stomach sank. I couldn't walk into my new boss' office with nothing written or nothing to show for it.

Dammit Harper! a voice in my head shouted.

"Maybe we can reboot it. Have you backed up anything to your drive?" Kathleen asked. "That's what I did since we don't have cloud server access yet."

"Drive? No, no, no. I-I keep everything written in Word." I fussed.

"Shame. You really should start backing everything up. Writer 101." Bryce clicked his mouse and the printer next to him began spitting out sheets of paper. Probably his article.

I was spiraling, trying to retrace my steps. Hunching under the table, I examined the cords and wires, all going in different directions. What could have happened? "I was right here writing it last week. Bryce, you were over there. Did the computers go out or something?" I shouted from under the table.

"I don't know man; I didn't see anything. This is the big leagues, Indy. How's that guy say? *Ohhh you gotta be quicker than that.*" Bryce grinned.

He was too jolly this was happening. I studied his face.

"He's lying, Indy. He's a whole lie and the truth ain't in him," a voice whispered in my head.

An icy shiver shot up through my back, and my ears rang. This was not happening.

Standing to my feet, I said, "Bryce. Did you do something?"

"Dude. Do what?" He had one hand in his pocket, and the other was holding his article.

"I forgot to log out. Did you. . . Delete it?"

"He did, Indy. He did!" another voice shouted.

I balled my fist and imagined slamming Bryce's head into one of those computers. It had to be him. This was not my first time at the rodeo and I was always careful. Something happened and it had to do with Bryce. The sinking feeling in the pit of my stomach told me so.

"Are you accusing me of something, Indy?"

"I told you to call me Indigo!" I fumed.

Tristan and Kathleen stood on either side of us, both of them carrying their articles. I wanted to snatch them, ball them up, and dunk them into the trashcan. If I was a cartoon character, steam would be screaming from my ears. Inching closer to Bryce, I stared him down. His face, with a smug smirk, told me all I needed to know. He had done something, and he knew I could never prove it. There were no cameras. This was

my fault just as much as it was his. He was upset that Harper placed my article on the front page instead of his.

Harper!

That fast, I had forgotten about her. She wasn't here anymore to back me up, and Bryce knew that. My eyes shot open, and I realized it. I was alone. I was alone in a den with the big bad wolf. But I could be a wolf too—if I had to be.

I looked at Kathleen and Tristan, almost pleading for help.

"Guys. We have to go in with Mr. John. Five minutes is up. Bryce, did you do something to Indy's article?" Kathleen asked in a soft voice. She wasn't sure herself, and the question hung in the air thick with confusion.

"Again. I had nothing to do with Indy's article. I resent the fact that I have even been accused. Some of us actually work hard and *actually* keep track of our work." Bryce gave a sinister smile.

Tristan stood off to the side, watching the group. "Kathleen is right. We have to get inside. I'm sorry about all this, Indy. You really should start backing up all your work." Tristan grabbed a laptop off the table and began backing away toward Mr. John's office.

"I need to use the bathroom," I said. "Tell Mr. John I'll be there in a couple minutes."

I stalked off and didn't wait for a response. *If he called me Indy, one more time.* . . I fumed. Pushing the restroom door open, I hurried into one stall and I sat on the toilet and covered my mouth with my hands. Screaming into my palms; angry tears made their way down my cheeks, and I was angry they were there and even angrier that I was crying at work. How could this have happened? My feet felt heavy, and I moved them around to get the blood flowing again. I was sweating at my temples and I held the sides of the stalls while I took deep breaths.

Bryce had something to do with this, and I knew he did. The voices confirmed it, but the look in his eye already told me what I needed to know.

I flushed the toilet and exited the stall, staring at myself in the mirror.

I hated my fucking hair. It was so short and I looked like a bewildered animal right now with it sticking up. I held my hand under the water, sprinkled water into my hair, and smoothed it down. My stomach was in knots and I almost ran back into the stall to empty the contents of my bowels—but I held back. I had to make it through this meeting with my new boss. Calling Harper one more time, she still didn't answer. Taking a few deep breaths, I checked myself in the mirror before making my way to Mr. John's office.

When I entered the room, everyone turned to stop and stare at me. There was a seat open next to Kathleen and she removed her purse and motioned for me to sit down. Tristan turned away, not making eye contact with anyone.

"Indigo. Nice of you to join us. Bryce tells me you had an article but had some sort of computer snafu. Does that mean you won't have anything to submit for the edition this month?"

I cleared my throat and tried not to glare at Bryce. "That is correct. Something, something happened to my computer, and it was deleted. I tried to retrieve it, but I couldn't find it anywhere," I said as calm as I could without my voice cracking. "I can rewrite it though. I, I don't remember everything, but I took really good notes. I can rewrite it tonight." I babbled.

"Mmmm." Mr. John tugged at his goatee. "What was your piece about? Is it something we absolutely need?" He held his breath and waited for my response. His eyes searched mine for reassurance, but my shaky pupils didn't catch the memo.

"It was about the *Black Feminist Nation*. An organization for. . . Black feminists—obviously. It was scheduled to appear

in their monthly newsletter as well. So I have to let them know too." I fumbled with my words. I scooted around in the leather seat next to his desk and it made an awful loud noise.

"Well, I'm sure we could do without it this week." He waved his hands and moved past me.

"May I suggest my article?" Bryce slid his pages across Mr. John's desk.

Tristan glanced at me from the corner of his eye.

"I'll have to review it later, but if it looks good with minimal corrections, we can add it for the cover."

Bryce beamed. He leaned forward in his chair and his eyes lit up. "The cover!? That would be great! Thanks!"

"We'll hash out the details later. But I wanted to get to know you guys a bit more. I don't have many notes from the previous supervisor, but from what I have been told, this unit needs help with procedures and systems. We have to become more consistent with creating content and it being released on a timed schedule. Since this is a paid internship, much more is required from you that your...ehhh. . . previous supervisor did not enforce. I have your log-in information for the Synergy House server cloud where you will save all of your work. Indy, please use this for all communication and documentation going forward."

Mr. John talked and talked for what seemed like hours, but I barely listened. He was going on and on about Harper and how unorganized she was. The higher ups brought him in to make change and bring stability to the unit. Just like that, he came into our lives and put an end to my article with the help of Bryce.

"And one last thing," Mr. John added from behind his—or Harper's—large desk. "The Synergy House Annual Retreat is still on in Driskill Mountains in a few weeks. Here are some forms to fill out. I checked your files and I didn't see any signed consents or demographic information." He rolled his eyes, jabbing at Harper once more. "Once these are completed, we can work out sleeping arrangements and food choices. I am looking forward to getting to know each of you, and I hope we can make up for lost time and start kicking out amazing content soon enough."

Bryce clapped, and an enormous smile spread across his face. This *would* excite him. He always had issues with Harper, and a new man coming in laying down the law was exactly what he wanted.

I looked at him like I was seeing him for the first time, really seeing him. I knew he had something to do with my article and this was his opportunity to make the front page. My hands gripped the sides of the seat as I pondered. I thought about Laylah Capri, and a lump formed in my throat so big I couldn't swallow. What would I say to her? How would she react? I was so excited to write this article for the BFN. She would probably see me as some disorganized college girl.

Maybe I was. Maybe I was.

CHAPTER NINETEEN

IT WOULD'VE BEEN easier to punch me in the gut. Maybe then I could take the pain. I could hobble over in surprise and when Laylah finished attacking me, we could go on like nothing happened. The look in her eyes today was worse, much worse. There are distinct times in someone's life when you know you've disappointed someone, and you have no good explanation why.

"So. . . you cannot do the article?" Laylah said at our BFN meeting.

I paused and took a spurt of breath. "My computer. . . it crashed or something. I-I I'm not sure what happened."

"You're not sure what happened?" Laylah side-eyed me. The room was quiet as the other feminist members stopped and stared. Their eyes darted back and forth between me and Laylah.

I squirmed in my seat. "I talked to my supervisor, and he said we might add it to the next edition, but that will be in three months." I winced like there was a physical blow to my body.

Laylah huffed and placed her hands on her temples and rubbed. "Okay, okay it's fine," she waved her hands. "We'll have to figure something else out. I was hoping your article

would lead us to program funding and help launch the new BFN high-school program. It's fine, Indy. What else do we have, ladies?" She turned and looked at the rest of the team for answers, boxing me out.

I remembered being in high school when I was the editor of my newspaper. I ran our meetings and I would cringe every time someone fumbled the bag with an article. This was my first time being on the receiving end and I didn't like it. "I'm sorry, I'm sorry." I mumbled. Now sweating.

"It's okay," Laylah said. "Mistakes happen." She gave me a sad smile. I wondered how many other fake, sad smiles she gave to people. I was sad I was on that list.

Yeah, a mistake, I fumed inside.

Bryce was on my next hit list and he didn't even know it. He hated the fact that Harper chose my work over his, and he made sure everyone knew it. Just this morning in our meeting he was bragging about how his article came to be on the front page where it should've been all along. Asshole. I never thought he would do something so underhanded. I had no proof, but intuition told me everything I needed to know. It had been a rough week.

"He has to be dealt with," a voice said in my head.

I agreed.

I sat through the rest of the BFN meeting in awkward silence, watching the clock on the wall creep by. Scrolling through my phone, I frowned when I saw three missed calls from Dad. I sat up, startled. Why would he call three times? Maybe it was something with one of the houses? I apologized again for the article and rushed out of the room like a cat with my tail between my legs.

"Indigo Tina Lewis?" My dad shouted into the phone.

My back straightened, and I stopped dead in my tracks in the Campus Center. He never called me by my full name.

"Yeah Dad, is everything okay?"

"Is your mom with you?" he asked quietly.

My eyes darted around, and my breathing quickened. We were silent for one second, two seconds, three seconds. . . How did he know? Did Minko Forrest know too? Should I lie? The seconds seemed so long as we were silent. If he knew the truth, maybe he could help.

"Yes, she is dad," I whispered, and all my shame expelled from my body.

"I thought so," he said in a hard tone. "I'm driving now, and I should be at your school in about ten minutes. Bring her with you," he commanded, and the phone disconnected.

I called Mom's cell phone, and she didn't answer. I called again and again and she still didn't answer! My hands were shaking and my stomach churned when I picked up the pace and hurried back to my room. When I got there and burst into the room, she was lying on her back, snoring her life away in my bed. Her bonnet covered her head, and she wore my eyepatches to sleep.

I shook her shoulders. "Mom, wake up! Wake up! Dad knows, and he's coming!"

"Daddy? Daddy?" Mom croaked out with her eyes still covered.

Dreams of Ez must've haunted her, too. It softened my tone. "Dad is here! He knows that you're here! He knows, and he wants us outside in ten minutes." I was rambling. How did he know? How did he know?!

"How does he know?" She panted. "We have to get Sidney." She planned her revenge against the Tunica Rivers Police Department less and less and treated our time together more like a vacation. I wondered if she even expected the detectives finding her. I tried splitting my time between school, Chaquille, and Mom, but she monopolized me these days.

"I don't know how he knows, but we have to get ready!" I rushed around the room and pulled clothes from my hamper. "Here, put this on." I said, shoving her a hoodie.

Mom ran into the bathroom, brushed her teeth, and snatched her bonnet off of her head. She shimmied into the sweatpants and hoodie and fixed herself in the mirror. "Do you have a little eyeliner? Some shadow I could put on my eyes?" she asked through the reflection in the mirror.

"Mom, we don't have time for that! We have to go!" I paced the room. I was spending so much time at Chaquille's room and hadn't been back here in a few days. When I opened my closet, Mom had collected packages of adult wet wipes. I gazed around and counted at least ten packages. "Mom, what is all this?"

"Oh, Sidney likes those. I got them for her."

"Where did you get the money?"

"I used that credit card from your purse."

"The one Daddy gave me?" I shouted.

"Yes, what's the big deal?"

"You can't just take my cards from my purse. That card is for emergencies, Mom! I didn't even know you took it. Give it back! Please . . ." I cried. My chest rose up and down and I paced around the room feeling like it was closing in.

"Indigo Tina Lewis, I haven't seen your father face-to-face in about five years now outside of Trochesse. I need make-up," she complained, completely bypassing me breaking down in front of her. Both of my parents had called me by my full name in less than an hour. Today was going great.

I stared at my mom. She and Dad were each other's first love. Back in a time when things were easier and fun. When the thought of him coming to pick her up and her rushing downstairs to meet him was exciting.

And now we were both terrified.

I rummaged through my make-up bag and tossed her some eyeshadow.

A few minutes later, Mom and I breezed past the so-called security guard in the front lobby. He cocked his legs up on the counter and barely noticed us from over the newspaper he was reading. Last year I felt like Mr. Chestnut had easy access to his students as the dorm rep. With Mom in and out of my room for days at a time with no one noticing anything; the security around this place was sorely lacking. A shiver went up my spine thinking about what else was going on in here Titus University knew nothing about. Maybe that would be my next article.

I spotted Dad's car in a distant corner of the parking lot. I watched Mom's shadow looming next to mine on the black top as we shuffled to him. She was walking slowly behind me, and she was quiet as a church mouse today.

She was never quiet.

Dad stepped out of the car, his eyes never leaving Mom. Standing behind the car door, he held it like a shield against someone or something. When we were finally in each other's space, Mom and I stopped walking and stood shoulder to shoulder with Dad's door in between us. I could smell his cologne from here. I bet Mom could, too.

"Hi, Benjamin," Mom said his name like she had said it a million times, a million different ways. It tasted different on her tongue every time she said it because now, she was different. This time his name tasted like her on the run with their oldest child in tow.

Dad stared between me and Mom, his hand still gripping the door. He stared her up and down, taking in the new crevices of her aging body. He flung the door closed and sprinted in Mom's direction. "Sonia . . ." He started. His voice was gruff, and he cleared his throat. His hand grazed her cheek, and he

stared into her eyes. Dad wasn't tall, and Ms. Arletha towered over him. Mom was shorter than Dad, and when he touched her face, she looked up at him in a way that told me God was real. Whatever they saw in each other's faces knew no limits, no bounds, and no restrictions. He studied her new features.

"What are you doing here? With Indy?" He gasped.

"They said they was taking me to New York City. They got another Trochesse or something like it up there. I told ya'll I wasn't going. So I ain't." Mom stepped back from Dad and squared off her shoulders.

"And you've brought Indy into this? She has enough to worry about. And now this! What are you thinking, Sonia?" Dad's arms were wide as he shouted.

I eyed the parking lot and exhaled a sigh of relief. No one was here to see our family drama.

"Dad. How did you know?" I gave a questioning stare.

"King . . ." He shook his head.

"Well, what do you want me to do, Benjamin? I will not go to no New York City where the rats are bigger than my head. I've been to that God awful place when I was touring with *The FatCats*. I can't live there." Mom stomped her foot. Her English accent had returned, to which Dad rolled his eyes.

"Sonia. People are looking for you. I will have to call the detective myself. You can't do this to Indy. To Sidney! She's already worried sick about Ez and now you too? I have let this go on long enough, but you will not continue to hurt my girls." Dad squeezed the cell phone in his hand. The car was still running, and he shut it off. "I'm calling Minko Forrest." He pressed a button on his phone when Mom slapped it out of his hand. Dad's phone fell to the ground and broke into pieces.

My eyes were wide as I watched my parents, who just minutes ago shared so much love between them with just glances, square off.

"Don't call anyone. Give me time. Give me some time to tie up things here. I will turn myself in, Benjamin." Tears welled in her eyes and she paced in place.

Seeing the tears in her eyes made my own eyes jumpy, and before I knew it, my face was wet too.

"No, Sonia! What if you get Indy in trouble?" Dad hissed. He took a step forward, and now he and Mom stood directly in front of each other.

"Benjamin. I would do nothing to put our dear daughter in danger. Dear daughter, in danger. Say that three times fast." Mom giggled, placing a hand to her mouth.

Dad found nothing funny, and he turned to me with disappointed eyes. "Indigo. You cannot handle everything on your own. When will you learn this?"

I dropped my head and shoulders, staring at the ground.

"You do what you need to do. I will give you three days. Get this taken care of, and your mom has to go in three days. Okay?"

I stared between my parents, feeling like cords connected the three of us. Dad was severing ties. Maybe I needed to too. Maybe he was right. "Three days, Dad. I haven't seen mom in forever. How about—"

"Indigo Tina Lewis, I said three days!" he shouted.

"Okay, Dad." I nodded. "Okay."

PART II
THREE DAYS

CHAPTER TWENTY

I PULLED THE BREAD out of the bag and tore a piece. "Mom! You have to figure something out! Did you see Dad's face? I've never seen him like that." My shoes made tracks in the dirt while I paced back and forth.

"Calm yourself down, young girl, calm yourself dowwwn-nn," Mom said, talking like she was a radio-host and I had just won a prize. "Your father is a punk and he ain't going to do nothing! We still ain't talked about what to do about this officer who took out Ez!"

"Mom, I don't care about any of that stuff." I sat down on the park bench.

Mom chased behind the ducks, throwing bread. "That's always been your problem, girl. Always worrying about something. Making tracks in the dirt like you're in a race."

I squinted up at Mom and caught a flash of amusement in her eyes. She was wearing a cowboy hat and a *Buffalo Bills* jacket. I took a sharp breath. "You know what, you are right about one thing. I am worrying about the wrong thing. You." I lashed. Grabbing my keys, I hopped off the bench and stomped to The Bus.

"We'll finish this conversation tonight, girl! You better be home by 8 p.m. and not a minute later! You ain't too grown!" Mom shouted.

My eyes shot around in case anyone was watching. I hoped someone heard her and they turned her in. *Home?* Where was home anyway?

I fired up The Bus and debris kicked up under my back tires while I peeled out. Banging on the steering wheel, I searched the furthest corners of my brain about what to do. About Mom? Yep. And Bryce? And Laylah? Yep, that too.

"Make it right."

"Do what you can, Indy. And as for Bryce. We will give him what he deserves."

"Go back there and pick up your Mama, girl!"

The voices rang out in my head at the same time.

If I didn't have to go to work, I would run back to my room and crawl under the blankets. I would shrink myself into a tiny ball and make an Indigo burrito as I tried to escape from it all. Signaling onto the highway, I thought about what to say to Bryce and the rest of the team. Mr. John alluded to a special investigative assignment in our last meeting and since then, Bryce had been glued to his side like white on rice. I shuddered to think what this team building retreat would look like. I cursed myself for agreeing to it in the first place, but it was Harper who set the whole thing up! "Ahhhh!" I screamed and pounded my fist against the steering wheel as the horn accidentally blared. A woman speeding up next to me on the left jumped in her car.

Why wouldn't Mom just listen? Dad wasn't weak, and he gave me three days to deal with this situation. That meant he trusted me and believed I could handle it. That meant something. I didn't want to disappoint him, and Mom was sho 'nuf cramping my style. I reached over the passenger seat into my purse and accidentally swerved into the next lane and the lady beeped her horn at me. "My bad! Charge it to the game!" I shouted at her through the window. Digging in the bottom of my purse, I found what I was looking for.

The detective's card. Minko Forrest. The one Trochesse hired to come look for Mom. I ran my fingers across the raised letters of his printed name and stared at his phone number.

I liked the man. But he was doing an awful job.

"Now, Indy. How could you?"

"Yea, Indy. Turn in your Mom? Where they do that at?"

"No, umph umph. That ain't even an option."

The voices disagreed with my thoughts, and somehow, I couldn't tell them from my own mind anymore. "Leave me alone!" I shouted out loud as I ripped into the Synergy House parking lot. Throwing the car in park, I snatched my books and fumbled with my purse. When I looked up, Kathleen was watching me frowning from her window.

"Oh. . . hey," I said, exiting the car and plastering a fake smile on my face.

"Girl? Are you okay?" Kathleen didn't waste any time. "I saw you screaming."

"I'm fine. I just had a rough day with my family. That's all." I sniffled and clutched my books to my chest.

"Okay. . . listen. I know you and I haven't been the closest since we started working here. But I have your back, girl." Kathleen kept up with my long strides. When I stopped walking, she almost ran into the side of me.

"Kathleen. Why?" I was side-eying everyone these days—including her. I didn't need any pity friends, so if that's why she was here, I would put a stop to it immediately.

"Well, it's just. I know we don't know for sure. But I think Bryce had something to do with your computer crashing. I mean, him and Mr. John are best friends these days and it would seem pretty convenient for your article to go missing."

My face softened.

Kathleen continued. "I'm just saying. If he can do that to you, what else is he capable of? I figured if anything, we got a story right here, so we better stick together." Kathleen's eyes were wide.

In true writer form, she was always curious and ready to report her findings. I started walking again—this time slower. "Okay." I nodded.

Minutes later, I scribbled in my notebook during our unit meeting with Mr. John and the rest of the team. Mr. John was tall and gave everyone hugs. His suits were tailored to every muscle, and he talked like he practiced talking in the mirror every night. I mean, he knew when to pause and look around for understanding. He would take a breath and keep on with his thought. He was precise and didn't have time for sob stories. He didn't care about the whys. He was about the bottom line and if the bottom line was to shape us into a formidable publishing house with a few, hungry writers to boot—that's what he was going to do.

He couldn't be more different from Harper.

Harper had left a mess, and he was a man who didn't take no mess.

"So Tristan, your article will be front page this month. Good work," Mr. John said and tossed Tristan an apple.

Tristan's cheeks blushed, and for half a second, he was handsome biting down on his apple.

"My man!" Bryce leaned over and pulled at Tristan's shoulder.

"And Kathleen. You will have the second page layout. Congrats to you!" Mr. John beamed and tossed Kathleen a banana.

Kathleen's eyes lit up while Mr. John gatekept like a mofo. And he tossed her a banana. A banana! How crass can you get. . . *wait*. . . *a banana*. . . I shot up in my seat as I had a great idea.

"Nice of you to join us, Indigo. I was wondering when you were going to perk up and grace the team with your presence." Mr. John interrupted my thoughts.

Clearing my throat, I said, "Sorry. I'm not feeling well."

"It's okay. I need you ready for next month. I know you're still upset about your missing article, but I need the fourth article ready for print." He mumbled it, like I was delicate. I wasn't delicate. I was soft—like a bomb.

"Understood." I scowled.

"Does that mean I'm doing something cool?" Bryce grinned.

"I saved something special for you, Bryce. I think you are going to be pleased. Actually, you can go wait in my office and I'll share the rest of the details with you shortly."

Bryce squealed in delight and put his fist to his mouth. He really sounded like a little pig.

I wanted to gut him like one.

The voices in my head giggled.

"Team. We have our assignments. Let's get to work." Mr. John instructed. He nodded at each of us, but me the longest.

CHAPTER TWENTY-ONE

RUSHING AROUND THE room, I tossed some clothes, clean underwear, and shoes into a bag.

"Are we going to get Sidney, too?" Mom's hands were on her hips.

"Mom, I don't know, I have to leave for my team building event in the Driskill Mountains. You can't stay here alone."

"Says who? Alone? I'm not a child. That young boy that sits guard downstairs? He ain't guarding nobody and nothing! I could give him something so good he'd feel like top flight!" Mom clamored.

"Indigo?" My body froze and I swear—for a second. My heart stopped.

"Chaquille. What are you doing here?" I instantly regretted giving him an extra key swipe.

Chaquille stood in the doorway gaping at my mom. His eyes never left her as he spoke to me. "We've been staying at my place for so long, you've been acting. . . funny. . . I wanted to see if something was up. This is what you are doing? Your mom?"

And there it was again. A hint of judgment that seared through my body like lightning.

"Chaquille, darling." Mom sauntered across the room, donning her famed English accent.

"Mhmm." She squeezed Chaquille's shoulder. Walking around, "Mhhmm," she said, squeezing his other shoulder. "He's a fine specimen of a man, Indy. You've done well my girl. You'll still need the spaghetti though!" Mom giggled.

I was still frozen in place. My words were caught in my throat and anything I remotely wanted to think, feel, or say felt like razor blade in my brains.

"Sit down here. Tell me more about yourself." Mom charmed. She pulled Chaquille into the foyer of my apartment.

Chaquille's attention darted between me and Mom as he plopped onto the couch. "Well." He started. "I'm from New York, and I DJ."

"Ohh DJ," Mom cooed. "Did Indy tell you I used to sing in a band? We were called The FatCats. I think you can figure out why we have that name. You've been with my daughter long enough." She snorted.

Chaquille chuckled and relaxed under Mom's spell.

So did I. I took a breath and sat down next to them.

After talking his ear off for an hour, Mom dozed off to sleep on the couch. I covered her with a blanket and crept back to my room with Chaquille hot on my heels.

"She's been with you all this time?" He glared at me. All the nice nice, kissy kissy faces him and my mom were making at each other not too long ago was gone and replaced with a scowl.

"Chaquille. I'm sorry. I . . I . . I didn't know how to tell you. I couldn't tell you. They were searching for her and they tried to keep it a secret and she came here. But she won't be here much longer. My Dad knows and he's going to turn her in. I didn't know what else to do." I wanted to cry. It felt like a moment where I would usually cry, and my body had some weird muscle memory reaction and my chest was tighter than

it's ever been. I was sure I was going to pass out. But I didn't. And I didn't cry. "I'm sorry." I stepped toward him.

Chaquille frowned and took a step back. "Indy, what do you want me to do? It's always something with you! I never know what you are thinking, and you keep secrets. *Big* secrets."

"I know. And you are right. You're right." I nodded.

I wanted to touch him. Slap him. Kiss him. Feel him. I trembled at the thought of Chaquille knowing the real me and yet—I never felt more exposed than in this moment. He burst through the doors, demanding answers and I hadn't anticipated him not wanting to be with me because of it. He loved the person I was longing to be. But I was also someone who had and would kill if necessary. I wanted to be *his*, Indy. I *would be* his Indy.

"I'm sorry, Chaquille." My voice cracked. I took one large step until I was directly in his face. I cupped his cheeks.

"No, Indy. This is not okay." He pulled away. "You turn into a different person when it comes to your mom."

"Well, what do you want me to do!" I exclaimed. I plopped down on my bed and crossed my arms.

"Indy. I told you before you can't do it all, baby. You have to let people help you. You have to start telling the truth." Chaquille knelt in front of me. His deep, amber eyes pierced mine while his hand caressed my thigh. I felt love, love, love.

I grabbed at Chaquille's shirt and pulled him in for a messy kiss. God, I loved this man. And I hoped he was ready for all of me.

CHAPTER TWENTY-TWO

BEFORE WE GOT on the road to the Driskill Mountains for our team building event, I made my way back to Tunica Rivers. I wanted to see Paisley, bad. It was amazing and weird. Just months ago, we were preparing for her arrival and now, none of us could see life without her. I wondered if my arrival when I was born excited Mom and Dad. I mean, I'm sure they were, but I was their *first*. The first born when they were teenagers. My mind kept replaying the way they looked at each other when we stood in a triangle the other day in the parking lot. Dad—longing for his past but tied to his future. Mom—always on the hunt for what's old and new. They both wanted different things, and they got it with me. But what did I want? Was I forever tied to their triangle by DNA, guilt, or something else? It always seemed like something pulled me back home. No matter how far I traveled, there was something magnetic that made it impossible for me to walk away completely. Not that I wanted to. I was as much Tunica Rivers as anyone else, but damn, did life back home have to be so hard all the time?

Pulling into the grocery store lot, I parked in the furthest space from the entrance, where no prying eyes could see. I had to check in on Sidney and then hop on the bus for the mountains.

I reached behind my seat and pulled the blanket down and whispered, "Mom. Wake up. We're here."

Mom, hiding under a large blanket, convinced me to take her to Tunica Rivers.

She had to be watched at all times, anyway.

She was snoring softly as the blanket brushed from her face. Her short hair was wild. She was hiding under hats and large sweaters, so she didn't draw attention to herself, but seeing her now with a slice of the sunlight gleaning against her face, she looked beautiful.

"Mom. Wake up. We're here." I repeated.

"What? King ain't no Martin Luther!" she said with a groggy voice.

"You're dreaming, Mom." I frowned and side-eyed her. *Why was she dreaming about King?*

"I have to run a few errands. Are you sure you're going to be all right if I drop you off here?"

She shot up in the car; her eyes red and squinty. "I'll be just fine. Some of my old band mates from *The FatCats* still live around here. I got me a bus schedule, and these legs. Have you seen these legs? They'll get me anywhere I need to go." Mom poked her thigh out from under the fluffy blanket.

I giggled. "I don't want to see them ham hocks, lady."

"Ham hocks!? Don't make fun of your mother, my dear. Sometimes we end up driving down the same road, just a different car."

"Well, make sure the car you are in has Wi-Fi so you can pick up the phone when I call you." I reached under Mom's side and pulled her cellphone tucked under her waist. "So this is it. After you . . Do what you do. . . You're calling the

police and letting them come pick you up, right? I confirmed. We rehearsed the plan in the car all the way here. She would visit a few friends and then turn herself in to Minko Forrest. Or so she said she would. The way her mouth was snarled up right now said otherwise.

She snatched the cell phone and rolled her eyes. "They will not tether me to these man-made things. Sometimes, I need to sing, and sometimes I need to swim. Both times I don't need no phone and I don't need no Minko." Mom folded the blanket and sat it on the seat beside her. She scoped out the scene and peered from the back window of The Bus before she hopped out of the back and trotted off into the sunset.

It would be the last time I would see her. I studied her womanly walk away from the car as she strutted her legs. I wasn't prepared for this moment, to watch her walk away from me, again. The last time this happened she was being carted off to jail. I guess this time she still was. It was better that way. I could drop her off, someone would spot her, and they would do the hard part for me. What I didn't have the courage to do quite yet, even with Dad's threats in my mind.

After I picked up a few items from the grocery store and lots of fresh produce for a dessert I wanted to make later, I left. When I turned right to take the ramp onto the highway, a voice said, *"Take your time, Indy. Go take care of what matters."*

I popped a U-turn and rode further out of town. If I was heading home, I would've already been there, but something wouldn't let me rest until I went to take care of what mattered.

When I turned down the familiar road, the weeping willow trees shrouded the street and created a canopy. I inhaled and smelled my home.

Pulling up, he opened the door and watched me get out.

"Hey, Will," I said with a nervous wave. My breathing was shallow.

"Hey, Indy." He smiled and held the door open.

That was a good sign.

"Nice to meet you." I heard another, softer, feminine voice. The door opened wider, and a petite girl with coppery skin and long, jet black hair stood next to Will and placed her hand on his shoulder.

"Indy, this is my girlfriend, Ashli." He beamed.

"Oh snap! Will has a girlfriend now! He didn't tell us that last time."

"Good for him."

The voices rang out in my head. I couldn't believe it. A girlfriend. When did this happen?

I licked my lips and chewed down on the inside of my cheek. "Um. Hi. I'm—"

"Indy. Yeah, I know. Will has told me all about his best friend." Ashli waved me inside.

Was I being set up? About to be jumped or something? She was being way too nice. And what exactly did Will tell her about me to think that she didn't see me as a threat to her relationship? Hell—a threat to her life?

"I'm not staying long. I was just in town from school and wanted to come and say hi to Will and his parents." I shifted my weight and looked down at their welcome mat. Was I welcomed?

"Aw shucks! Indy! It is so good to see you again!" Mrs. Simms said from behind Will and Ashli. "You come inside this house and say hello to us. Ain't no just stopping by here."

I smoothed my shirt, took a deep breath, and walked inside. "I can't stay long. I have groceries in the car and I don't want them to spoil." I motioned to my car. My hands were shaking as Ashli looked me up and down. His parents caught us kissing and now they were bosom buddies with Ashli. Family would always side with family.

"Nonsense. Go get those groceries and bring them into this house while you visit."

Ashli and I spent the next two hours sizing one another up. She and Will sat next to each other, and she placed her legs over his when they sprawled in front of the tv. I thought it would make me jealous, and in some ways, I guess it did. That could have been us, but I'm not sure if I truly believed that. I loved Chaquille. For what I needed right now in my life, he was my breath of fresh air. He was my lighthouse on a dark and stormy night. It calmed my spirit to see Will happy, and with someone who cared about him and could return his feelings when I couldn't.

"So Indy." Ashli leaned over after Will hustled to the bathroom. She and I were alone in the living room. "Will told me you left him in New Orleans."

I swallowed. She dropped the nice girl act and got straight to the point.

"Yes. I was wrong about the way things played out last year. That is why I'm here now." Looking Ashli straight in the eye, I hoped she saw my sincerity.

"You know. He has a soft spot for you. He speaks of you often. . . We are together now, and I hope you respect that." Ashli muttered.

"I understand what you're saying, Ashli. I mean no disrespect. I just want my friend back, too." And I meant it. I was just happy that Will was even speaking to me right now. If he was happy, I wanted him to be.

Ashli stared at me for a long time as Wheel of Fortune blared in the background. "Okay." She nodded. "I don't want any drama."

"I come in peace." I waved my hands.

"Of course you do, Indy." Mrs. Simms breezed into the living room carrying to-go containers. "Here is your food, and the rest I packed up for you to take home to your family and for your trip. You have fun now. Those Driskill Mountains

are cold at this time of the year." She shivered in place. Deep laugh lines creased her face, and I wondered why she couldn't be my mom.

"Thank you, Mrs. Simms." I gave her a hug.

Will carried the food and containers outside and loaded them into the trunk.

"Thank your mom again for cooking. She bust open my groceries and just took over. She is the best."

"You ain't got no business trying to cook nothing, Indy." Will threw his head back and laughed. I didn't find his comment funny, but I laughed too.

"Keep your head up, Indy. You're the strongest person I know. Ez is always with you," Will said. Staring into his eyes made my heart skip a beat. Ashli watched us from the front window. I saw why she felt the need to have a conversation with me about our friendship. I saw what she saw. And what Mrs. Simms saw.

Will still loved me.

My mind was heavy with thoughts of Will as I drove in the direction of home. Lights, signs, and other cards whizzed by me, but I was in a daze. I was stopped at a red light when my phone rang and I read four letters.

"King," I said, coolly.

"Listen, I'm sorry for not getting back you sooner, I'm getting ready to go on tour and it's been crazy trying to prepare for it. Anyway, your dad told me that Sonia is with you?"

I swallowed. I messaged King so many times trying to get more information about Mom, and now he wants to show up at the last possible moment? Fuck that. "Why didn't you tell me Mom was back? She came to you first! How are you going to be there for Sidney if everything comes before her?" Cars beeped behind me as the light turned green. I took a sharp left and pulled The Bus into an empty parking lot. "You don't even know Sidney!" I yelled into the phone.

"Indigo, she was talking crazy. She mentioned taking Sidney and the three of you running away. She called you rebels. Said you guys were going to kill a cop or something to get them back for Ez. I had to tell your dad. I should've told him from the beginning, but like I said, I was planning for the tour." King got quiet for a second, his voice turned lower. "And as you said, I always put things before Sidney."

I bit down on my lip. Mom told him about the cop thing before she mentioned it to me.

"Indigo, Sidney doesn't want to live with me. I don't want to force her to be anywhere she doesn't want to be. But you always have a soft spot for your mom. You are like her little secretary. You do everything she tells you. I thought if she told you to take Sidney away—you would."

I clenched my jaw so tight my teeth shook in my mouth. King didn't even know me. I was running around trying to protect Sidney, Mom, everyone else, and yet—King thought that he had to protect Sidney from me.

From me.

He thought my love for Mom was a weakness, not a strength.

I lowered my shoulders from my ears. "What are you saying, King?"

He was thoughtful for a moment; I could hear him breathing and thinking through the phone. "I want Sidney to be happy, and only she can decide where that is. But Indy, you have to let her go," King whispered. "Let your mom. . . go."

Sidney was in her bedroom napping. I sat down beside her and the bed sank. I stroked her hair.

"Hey, little sis." I smiled.

"Indy Lindy!" Her eyes sprang open. She was excited to see me, and that warmed my hardened heart.

I didn't want to fight anymore. I didn't want Sidney to feel like she had to choose.

"Sidney . . ." I swallowed. "If you want to live with your dad. It's okay. I understand."

Sidney buried her face into her pillow and huffed. "It's just. . . hard being here. All I do is think about Ez. And you're away at college. It's like. What is here for me? What do I have? But I don't want to go either. I don't want to leave you guys." Her eyes filled with tears that dripped onto her pillow.

My heart wrenched, and I wanted to scoop her into my arms, rock her back and forth, and tell her everything would be okay. Because it would be okay. I would make sure of it. These are the times when I found myself the most mad at Mom. She was missing for the moments when Sidney needed a woman's touch. She had Ms. Arletha, but Sidney still felt like an outsider since King was her real dad and Mom was gone. Sidney was low-key depressed and she didn't have the words for what we both didn't fully understand. I was trying to understand her in a way that was new to me.

"Let's go take a ride." I pulled the blankets back from the bed.

She frowned. "Go where? I'm chilling, Indy." She whined.

"C'mon." I tossed some clothes slung over the hamper in her direction.

A few minutes later, Sidney and I crept up to the inlet where I had dispersed Ez's ashes months earlier.

Sidney was quiet as we walked over the sandy marsh and smelled the stench of fish and mud. She peered around, almost like she was searching for Ez. I knew the feeling.

"He's here." I smiled. "I feel him everywhere. He's always with you, Sidney. You just have to believe that he is. He's right here." I pressed Sidney's chest.

I gazed out over the horizon and cursed the police for killing Ez and doing this to our family. For forcing us to move forward from a man we believed to be larger than life. He was our life. "Just give it some time. Make your own decision." I grabbed my sister's hand and held it.

The waves crashed around us, proving that things could be made new again. Sidney could be made new again, and so could I. We would get through this as a family. I had to make sure Mom and Sidney were safe. No one got left behind. Unless I had to do it myself.

CHAPTER TWENTY-THREE

PLACING THE CONTAINER Mrs. Simms made into the trunk with the rest of the coolers and food, I pulled down the door to the van and popped my earbuds into my ears. Hopefully Kathleen, Bryce, Mr. John, and Tristan were the type of people that recognized when someone had their buds in and didn't want to speak. I was hoping for a quiet two-hour ride to Driskill Mountains and getting this weekend over and done with so I could focus on what to do about Mom.

"Dude, aren't you tired of sitting in the back?" Bryce looked back at Kathleen, while she ducked and made her way to the third-row seat in the Synergy House van.

"Excuse me?" Kathleen sucked her teeth.

I pressed my buds tighter into my ears, willing myself to un-hear that.

"Not cool, Bryce?" Tristan frowned.

The van hummed softly as we waited for interns from the other teams to board. Mr. John's jeans were pressed with a stiff crease in the middle and a tight ball cap hugged his head. He nodded, waved, and took a few pats on the back as he huddled

with the other intern supervisors and eyed their worker bees in the van windows.

I wondered what kind of nonsense we were in for.

Glancing out the window every few minutes, I flopped between reading—writing an article that I kept scribbling out because it didn't seem quite right—and shaking my head at the next outlandish thought that came out of Bryce's mouth. Somehow, we made it up the mountain. The higher in elevation we rose, the chillier the air became. I searched my duffel bag and pulled my fleece sweater over my head.

"You were thinking ahead. I just brought my little jacket." Kathleen eyed my fluffy savior.

"Don't worry, I have a huge blanket I packed away too." I half-smiled.

"Here. Have some." Kathleen beamed back at me and shoved some Twizzlers in my direction.

"Thanks." I tugged on a stringed piece and chomped down; my stomach stirred.

We hit a pothole, and the van lurched forward. Bryce and Tristan were in the middle row asleep, and they jumped at the jolt.

"I always crave sweets when it's time for Aunt Flo." Kathleen bit into another Twizzler.

"Aunt Flo?"

Her eyes widened. "Yeah like. That time of the month?"

Choking on candy, my cheeks flushed red. "Oh. . . I never heard that before."

Kathleen cackled and before long, we giggled together.

When the van finally stopped, I checked my phone. When I saw a big X in the right corner, my heart skipped a beat. We had no service at the top of Driskell Mountains.

"I think you guys have noticed by now that there is no service. This isn't by accident. We like for our teams to bond,

and so we only have one land line in each of the cabins. All other service is restricted. The idea is to turn inward and learn each other and ways to work better as a team," Mr. John said with sleepy eyes. His shirt was wrinkled, but the crease in his pants remained, even after a road trip.

Bryce darted around the wooded area, placing his phone to the sky and frowning. "There can't be, like, no service. This is crazy."

Tristan was still half-asleep and his eyes were red.

"Bryce, you can always use the landline in your room. Here are your keys, everyone." Mr. John handed out an old school golden key.

Kathleen and I were sharing a cabin for the weekend and after the drive up we had, I was actually looking forward to it. We were to unpack and then meet in a few hours for the first activity of the night followed by a late dinner.

When we entered the cabin, I gasped. The panels were a dark shade of brown and the floors were new hardwood. In the corner there was a twin bunk-bed set and when I pressed the mattress, it felt soft and didn't squeak.

"Check this out." Kathleen poked her head out of the bathroom. When I peeked inside, my neck twisted around, gawking at the white marble countertops and glassed-in showers.

"Whoa." I breathed.

"Whoa is hella right," Kathleen said.

"So, what do you want to do?" I relaxed my shoulders. The mountain smelled different, and my lungs felt opened.

"I think the guys are bringing in all the food and supplies. We're good for the next few hours. Want to go for a walk?"

I nodded and inhaled the rich wood. Kathleen was speaking my language right now.

"We're going for a walk, guys." Kathleen zipped her jacket and shouted over her shoulder. The boys were unloading the truck and placing the coolers of food in the cabin with the supervisors.

"Here, take this." Mr. John tossed me a heavy flashlight.

I peered up at the setting sun through the tall, slender trees. They seemed to go higher and higher until I couldn't make out the tops.

"This is amazing." Kathleen gushed and took in a deep breath.

Wet leaves crunched up my boots, and the dirt smelled wet. I had to agree, this was pretty cool.

"So, what do you think about Mr. John?" Kathleen leaned in with a devilish smile.

I snorted. "I think we're in for a rude awakening."

"I know, man." Kathleen shivered. "Have you talked to Harper?"

I thought about 'ol Harper Sullivan, and I didn't know what to feel. It took Harper about three days to call me back after we found out that they replaced her. When I went to see her at the theater where we both used to work together, she was back at work.

"I was in over my head, anyway." She waved me away. *"I can't let those trivial things stress me out. I have this place to take care of. You know Rita still can't run the theater without me!"* She rolled her eyes.

I swallowed and didn't pry. I wanted to tell her about Mr. John. About Bryce and my missing article. I wanted her to commiserate with me, at least for a few minutes. As she buzzed around the theater performing tasks she did for years and years, I realized she didn't want to hear about it. She already moved on—or moved back. I couldn't move back. There was no reason for me to, and so I changed the subject.

"I've talked to her." I started slow. "She seemed like she's already on to the next thing."

"How long do you think Mr. John will last?" she asked.

The sun was just descending from the sky and I wondered how many more hours of light we had. "I don't know. He seems pretty comfortable, especially with Bryce." I palmed leaves on a shrub as we brushed by, making our way through the carved path.

"Right? I thought him and Mr. John were going to suck each other's dicks after Mr. John gushed about Bryce's article about that dead coach."

I sucked in a blast of air and choked on Kathleen's words. "How do you know he's dead?"

"I mean, that's probably it? Everyone thinks he's dead. With everything he was into and all the girls they say he was messing with, what else could have happened?"

"I guess you're right." I held back a smile. Hearing Kathleen's theory, I mean, he really had done it to himself. Sometimes being a feminist wasn't pretty, and it was definitely a be-hind-the-scenes job, and I was up for the task. I just wished Theodora saw it that way. The more her and I talked about Mr. Chestnut, the more we disagreed about him.

"I'm glad you're here, Indy."

"I'm glad you're here too."

Maybe we could be friends. Just maybe.

CHAPTER TWENTY-FOUR

"**Y**OU GUYS HAVE to lean back. The point of this exercise is to trust each other." Mr. John chuckled. When I looked down, I peed a little. I was at least ten feet in the air on top of a raised wooden platform. Everyone else went first, falling back with their arms crossed and eyes closed, while the rest of the team locked arms and stood below to catch the falling person.

Sounded like some bullshit to me.

"I can't. I can't do it!" I yelled below. Blinking a few times, I was eye level with some trees and that made my stomach fall even harder.

"C'mon, Indy. We're trying to eat dinner at some point tonight!" Bryce shouted.

It was only a couple of minutes I was up here. Everyone else didn't have any issues turning around, closing their eyes, and damn near jumping off a cliff. Even Kathleen didn't struggle as much. Peering over the ledge, I looked down and gulped. When you didn't have the luxury of just trusting someone was there to catch you, these cutesy team building games seemed like jumping into the pits of hell.

"Indy, you can do it!" Kathleen screamed. "Just close your eyes. I got you!"

"I can't. I can't!" My mouth watered, and I swallowed away the spit threatening to turn into bile.

"Indigo! The point is to trust us. You have to trust us. We will catch you! Right team? Tell her! Encourage her! Show her! She has to feel supported. We support you, Indigo!" Mr. John yelled. I watched the veins in his neck pop out as he screeched into a bullhorn.

"*You can do this, Indy. You can take care of yourself. Safe and protected, honey. Safe and protected,*" Mom's voice said in my head.

I looked up at the skies and noticed the twinkling stars. I wondered what Mom was doing, right here, right now, in this moment. She wouldn't *believe* what I was doing.

"Safe and protected," I whispered to myself, looking over the ledge. "Safe and protected."

"Hurry up, Indy! We're starved!" Bryce barked.

"Safe and protected. Safe and protected. I am safe and protected," I repeated. "And Bryce, it's Indigo!" I said, as I took a breath, closed my eyes, and tumbled backward into support.

Seconds later—and I mean seconds—they gathered us around a campfire, dishing out food and treats. I warmed my hands against the orange flames and hoped they didn't see my warmed cheeks too. I felt silly enough already. The supervisors dragged out the coolers full of food and they set up the picnic tables with subs, cold cuts, fruits, pies, and other snacks donated by the Titus cafeteria crew.

"Now, this potato salad is excellent. Who made it, Indy or Kathleen?" Bryce grinned and white pasty food swirled in his mouth.

Whatever good vibes I had from conquering a fear disappeared while I shifted on the tree stump I was sitting on and cocked my head at Bryce. Was this guy fucking serious?

"Dude, seriously, what is your issue with the ladies?" Tristan shot out. He was sipping from a silver flask and whatever was inside had his eyes low, and tolerance for Bryce even lower.

Tristan never defended me or Kathleen against Bryce's side remarks.

The moon was sitting full and high in the sky. When I peered up, the stars were twinkling. Ez used to always say when the moon was full, people showed their truest colors. I thought it was just Ez talk, being as though his monthly ritual was baying at the moon in his canoe on Tunica Rivers; but the way Bryce spewed venom and the usual quiet Tristan barked back, I wondered more about Ez's theory.

"Bryce, you're an asshole." Kathleen said blankly.

My eyes shot around as I passed around a cheese platter and cracked open the container Mrs. Simms made me before I left her house.

"Excuse me?" Bryce frowned. The bonfire Mr. John spent an hour building started crackling in front of us. "You sound like my ex. You can't be easy on the ladies, Tristan. They have that whole feminism thing to their advantage. Jam you up in anything."

Kathleen gasped. "So now we're feminists because we don't put up with your shit?"

Tristan took some potato chips, scooped a large wad of pudding, and shoved it into his mouth. "Well, she's not wrong." He passed the food to Bryce.

Bryce grabbed a serving spoon and scooped seconds of everything onto his plate and new desserts we just pulled out of the cooler. "You're taking the ladies' side? C'mon man, you guys know I'm just joking. Besides. In order to get what you want; you have to be able to take the heat. I don't mind playing the bad guy sometimes." He looked around and genuinely appeared confused.

That would be a fleeting face as I watched him eat, knowing what was to come.

"Anyway. Bryce, what's this top secret article Mr. John has you working on?"

Bryce's face broke into a half-smile, and he sat his plate down on a rock. "I can't tell you much about it, but it's way better than that coach article."

"What's better than a missing coach?" I asked. I was careful not to say *dead*.

He giggled and leaned his head back. "This is real writing, Indigo. You know, the kind you actually have to prepare for, do research."

"And what is it I do?" I retorted. Was this a jab at me? Was I taking this personally? Everything this man said had a double meaning, and it was exhausting.

"Oh, I meant nothing by it." He shook his head and sipped from the flask Tristan slipped to him. "No need to get sensitive." He threw his hands in the air in a defenseless "don't shoot" motion.

I sighed and watched Bryce eat, waiting for the moment it would happen. Watching someone eat was akin to watching paint dry. It took too damn long to get to the finish line.

A few minutes later, the fireworks started.

Bryce scratched his neck. "Dude. It's hot tonight." He fanned his t-shirt.

"Hot? It's chilly at night. What are you talking about?" I questioned. Playing my part was key.

"Seriously, Bryce, it's the flask you were just chugging down." Kathleen rolled her eyes. She leaned back and gazed up at the stars.

Bryce said nothing but ran his fingernails down his throat and chest. "No, I'm hot." He blinked a few times.

"Shut your mouth then! Blowing out all that hot air!" Kathleen joked.

Bryce dug his nails into his arms. "No seriously guys. I'm hot as shit." He panted.

"Are you okay?" Tristan asked. He leaned in past the fire and peered at Bryce. Bryce jumped up from his seat and stormed to a girl from one of the other units who was in charge of the food.

"What was in that food?" Bryce shouted at her.

"Huh?" she asked with a giggle. The girl sitting next to her tucked a water bottle with something that clearly wasn't water into her jacket. They were also feeling the effects of something, and it was making her giddy. Was everyone here tipsy on the low? My plan was working out even better.

"What was in the food? Any bananas?" He hurled his words at her.

The girl's eyes darted back and forth as she giggled again. "Dude. What are you talking about?" She held onto her stomach and fell out laughing.

This is gonna be a piece of cake, Indy! the voices in my head screamed in unison.

Kathleen, Tristan, and I watched Bryce stomp in place, and within mere moments, he was clutching his throat. "Bananas. Something had bananas!" He coughed and his neck turned red. It was seconds before he face-planted into the dirt and was on the ground shaking.

He was down like Frazier.

CHAPTER TWENTY-FIVE

BRYCE LAY, WRITHING on the ground; his legs kicking up wood chippings around him.

"Mr. John! Mr. John!" Kathleen screamed. Her food dropped to the wet earth beneath her while she yelled his name.

"What's happening here? Is he allergic to anything? Does he have an EpiPen?" Mr. John barked out questions and orders.

"He carries an Epi-Pen and an inhaler!" Kathleen jumped up and down. She leaned against a tree and let out a strangled sob.

Tristan, clearly buzzed, said through slurred words. "He's allergic to bananas. Remember Harper, Indy? This shit is B-A-N-A-N-A-S," he sang.

I didn't remember a thing.

"Mr. Rullan! Go find Bryce's Epi-Pen if he has one! Someone call 9-1-1! Now!" Mr. John shouted.

"Ugh shit! I don't have service!" Kathleen screamed.

"Go to the landline in one of the cabins! Move!" Mr. John demanded. His hair was out of place and pants were wrinkled now.

Tristan scampered in the direction of his cabin. His silver flask had him walking sideways and immensely slow. Bryce lay writhing on the ground as a smashed crowd formed around him. I inched closer to his body to watch his demise.

"Someone call 9-1-1!" a girl shouted.

"There's no cell service, remember!" someone else replied.

I remembered that part the most. I read it in the welcome packet all the way at the bottom in fine print that everyone else skirted over. I recalled the slights Bryce had subtly attacked me with. The underhanded jokes. The comments about The Bus. The ultimate betrayal. My article.

He dared to fuck with me like this girl wasn't the monkey on his back who refused to leave.

I smirked. Kathleen had tears in her eyes watching Bryce fight for his life after our team building exercise.

We had built a team all right.

Only he wasn't part of it anymore. Teammates didn't disrespect each other. Teammates didn't purposely delete articles. He started this. He chose violence—and unfortunately for him—violence chose me a long time ago.

The low music that was playing from someone's Bluetooth speaker stopped and everyone stood around Bryce's body watching the show. What felt like hours was really seconds, and my eyes danced with excitement. The light from Bryce and Tristan's cabin was on, and Tristan was in there rummaging around. I squinted and could make out the landline phone on the wall. Tristan stumbled around the room, in the opposite direction.

"Cmon Bryce! Don't do this. Don't do this to us!" Mr. John leaned over Bryce and banged on his chest.

Bryce's chest was once rising fast and high. Now it was low and shallow. Bryce stopped shaking, and his eyes were glassing

over. They were darting in different directions and when they caught mine; I had to choke back a snort.

"Our girl came up with this one all by herself!"

"Go Indy, way to take the lead!" the voices congratulated me.

My heart swelled with pride. When I stopped by Will's house earlier today, I had already purchased what I needed to make Mama Jackie's famous Nana Pudding.

Extra Bananas.

I asked could I keep my groceries in Mrs. Simms' refrigerator so they wouldn't spoil sitting in the car when she insisted I come inside. She saw the ingredients she said, *"somebody is making them some pudding."* I smiled, so I didn't incriminate myself.

When she offered to make it for me, I sat back and got to know Ashli, and let Mrs. Simms do the hard part for me. And when I slipped it into the coolers with the rest of the packed food provided by the Titus University culinary team and passed it around for everyone, I knew entitled Bryce wouldn't think twice about what he was putting in his mouth.

"What is taking Tristan so long?" a supervisor yelled.

"Wait! Wait! Where is his Epi-Pen? I think he travels with one?" A girl ran up to the campsite.

"I don't know but I'm losing him someone *else* call 9-1-1!" Mr. John howled.

"Wait! Shit! Just use mine. I have an Epi-Pen too. Use mine!" An ugly ass boy with buck teeth and too many freckles from the marketing department rummaged through his bag and shoved Bryce's saving grace forward.

My internal smile faded away. "Can you use someone else's Epi-Pen?" I asked. This couldn't happen. They couldn't save him. It was too late.

Mr. John was silent as he snatched the pen from the boy—popped the cap off—and jammed it into Bryce's arm. Bryce lay motionless for a few seconds, and we stood silently around him.

Only the snap of the fire was heard, and even the bugs were silent. Was he dead? I waited with bated breath. He had to be.

Answering my question, Bryce's body jerked and shook, and he began coughing and grasping at his throat.

"He's alive! He's alive!" Mr. John screamed.

The air left my chest and my fists balled. This motherfucker was *alive*.

The crowd that formed around Bryce peered down at him. Some with tears in their eyes, all with their hands over their mouths in shock.

Except for me.

Bryce couldn't speak, and his eyes danced around at everyone. His face found mine and his eyes narrowed and darkened. This mother-fucker lived.

Did he know? He couldn't know.

He held my gaze as my heart drummed. We shared knowledge between us two. We both knew what we knew and didn't know exactly what the other knew. But we *knew*.

The game was on.

CHAPTER TWENTY-SIX

CHAQUILLE STUFFED FRENCH fries into his mouth. "What's wrong with you?"

My hands shook under the table, and I shoved them under my thighs. My palms were sweating and I wiped them onto my pants.

"Bryce," I whispered.

"Indy, that's not your fault." Chaquille's face flattened.

He was trying to make me feel better. Any other day, it would have been cute.

Today it was ugly. So ugly.

My phone buzzed and when I swiped up, Mr. John emailed our unit and canceled work for the next few days until they properly inspected the food to ensure the only thing poisonous was bananas. Could never be too sure in a world where coaches disappeared into watery graves, and they burned boys in incinerators.

"Bryce." My chest seized, while my eyes scanned the email.

"Seriously, Indy. Relax. You're taking this really personal." Chaquille's lips thinned.

Bryce survived. Mr. John saved him with one swift jab at the forearm. The air in his chest seemed to re-inflate him, and he puffed back to life. His eyes were dark and woefully stared at me. And that boy! Offering up his own Epi-Pen, dammit! My miscalculations had caused me to lose a body. Not only was I furious about Bryce's ass, but I was planning to call Minko Forrest to make sure mom turned herself in. I chewed on my fingernails as shards shot across the table.

"Antsy, are we?" Chaquille took a sip of his soda and eyed me.

"I don't feel good. I have to go." I slapped my hands against the table and scooted out of the booth seat.

"Indy, wait!" Chaquille shouted. "I have something for you." He wiped his mouth and chased me out the door.

I hurried my pace and ran full sprint out of the cafeteria with tears blurring my vision. "Excuse me!" I choked, slamming into someone walking in my path.

Chaquille grabbed my arm and pushed a small box in my direction. "Here. I was going to give this to you at some super special moment. But you're always on the move these days and you barely let me come over to your place. So, I had to improvise. Isn't this romantic?" He looked around and chuckled.

I fingered the small box in Chaquille's hand and opened it. The scowl sitting on my face fell flat, and my breath was ragged. I held up Ez's dog tags. The ones Mom and I found in his box of belongings. They were shiny, cleaned, and hanging from a necklace. I fastened the clasp around my neck and a blush touched my cheeks. They felt warm resting against my heart.

"I hope you don't mind. You were going on and on about them when you came home from Tunica Rivers. I thought you might like to keep them with you all the time." Chaquille closed the gap between us and whispered. "It's the darkness, Indy. I know it gets you down sometimes. But the darkness

could teach us things the light never could. If we let it. I love you. I am here for you. Please let me be."

"I love you too, Chaquille." I said, resting my hand against his chest. And I did, I really did.

After I took a nap, I was up looking crazy, still wrecking my brain about this thing with Bryce and where I went wrong. I pulled on my sweater and gulped through a dry throat. The look on his face told me he knew I tried to take him out. Surely, he would tell the police what I did and they would come and arrest me. Maybe when I called Minko Forrest for Mom, I should turn myself in too. It was genetic anyway—the crazy. Was that even possible? That I was crazier than *thee*, Sonia Lewis? Couldn't be. I wasn't even capable of carrying out a *planned* murder. Three days were up, and I had already avoided two phone calls from Dad. I was sure he was probably on his way here now.

Pulling myself under my blanket, I smelled Mom's scent against my pillow. On cue, she slid into the room in my slides. "Dear daughter, what is the matter?"

Hiccups escaped my throat and when I came up for air from under the blanket, Mom's weight sank in the bed beside me, and she stroked my hair. I grabbed onto the towel wrapped around her soft skin. "What are you doing here?" I shrieked.

"My dear daughter, I never left." She cupped my face.

I didn't ask any more questions or even know where she slept. I didn't want to fight with her anymore.

I told her everything including why it was time for me to call Minko Forrest. I had to focus on my studies and Chaquille. I couldn't kill a cop, and I definitely didn't want to bring Sidney into this mess. Through clenched eyes and hot

tears, I blubbered on. My mom learned about Bryce and what a terrible person he was and how he had to go. He deleted my article. I showed her the dog tags Chaquille gave me, and what he said about the darkness teaching us things the light never could. I wept about Will. I told it all.

Mom patted my head with her wet shower hands. She was quiet, but something flashed in her eyes that I hadn't fully considered.

We were more alike than anyone. She and I. Me and her. I was supposed to be Indigo Barre, but Mom insisted her girls be like her and carry the Lewis name. Sonia Lewis. Indigo Lewis. Sidney Lewis.

We were two sides of the same coin.

All of my good and bad swam somewhere in my body, firing off synapses that coursed through Mom's body too. We shared the same DNA—and by the looks of it—we *really* shared the same DNA.

And that was a darkness that had yet to be realized.

"Honey. Look at me." Mom grabbed my damp, puffy face. "You get yourself together. I need you here with me. Listen to me carefully, I am not going back to Trochesse, okay? And ol' what's his name, Mink Tree? He can kiss my whole ass! They will have to chase me down before I let them take me."

"Mom, what do you mean?" I pleaded. "This is the only way."

"I am saying I'm not going. Let's go on a road trip! Take The Bus and drive cross-country."

"Cross country?" I raised an eyebrow.

"Yea baby. Cross-country. Later for these men! They don't respect us. They don't know what we need or how to get the job done. If they are going to haul you in for trying to poison that boy, well, they'll have to catch you first! Just like they'll have to catch me!" Mom's face was stern. She cupped my chin, waiting for my response.

"Mom. . . I. . . I. . ." I licked my lips. "I can't go away. I have midterms coming up. And I can't take time away from Synergy House like that. And—"

"And what, Indy? You worry about the wrong things, my girl." Mom shook her head and released my chin as she tightened the towel around her body. Water pooled at her feet. "You have to live a little more. I hope you didn't think I would ever let you hand me over to that Tree man. The world is a big place and if you keep looking, you'll find more Bryces and more Jaxons. Sometimes the trash takes out itself."

Mom said the last sentence in her English voice and paddled back to the bathroom, shaking her head behind me.

The trash took itself out.

Bryce was the trash.

Maybe Mom was right. If they were going to take me in, it wouldn't be quietly. If they wanted to come and lock me up behind what I did to Bryce, well—I wouldn't make it easy for them.

Standing to my feet, I studied myself in the mirror. I skimmed my jaw with my fingertips and stared at my short hair. I was always that girl. That girl with the braids. The braids that Jaxon cut off. The braids that a man grabbed before I ended his life in New Orleans.

I smoothed a few loose hairs and my eye twinkled. It didn't look half bad. When my mom wasn't wearing her hair store wigs, we could pass for sisters.

I wouldn't let them take her away. To hell with Minko Forrest.

"Mom!" I shouted, not moving from the mirror and my reflection. "Let's do it. Let's go on a road trip. You and me."

CHAPTER TWENTY-SEVEN

MOM SQUEALED WITH delight. "Eeek! We're really doing this, girl. Me and you. It will be better this way. You know your stanking daddy will worry. Doesn't he have one of those tracker things on the phone? We don't want him chasing us down while we go on our adventure." She danced in the seat.

I held down the side button to power it down.

I was sitting in the passenger seat and Mom was driving. I looked her up and down. She wore a short black wig she picked up from the consignment shop and the mole right above her right lip gawked back at me as she gnawed on pork rinds. She fired The Bus through the bible belt. Mom had picked up some pounds since she started camping out in my dorm room.

I hoped it was happy weight.

We were on an adventure. I checked out the signs on the highway as we whizzed by, urging people to find themselves in church. What were people looking for when they went to

church? Mama Jackie was a stocking wearing—pearl clutching—candy in her purse—carrying woman. When Sidney and I went with her, she ushered us and others to our seats. She took her job seriously, pointing people to their assigned sections with a stern face and bobbing down the aisle. But when we left church for the day, she spoke of spirits, dreams of fishes, and where the moon sat in the sky. When the moon was full, she kept a close eye on Ez. She said it made him crazy. What was it that made this family crazy? And who was the keeper of what made up crazy?

Before we left, I sent Mr. John an email and told him I had a family emergency and would need a few weeks off from work. I didn't even check to see if he responded or not; there was nothing that would stand in the way of what Mom and I were here to do—whatever that was. Chaquille said he didn't understand and shook his head in confusion. I knew he would call my dad, but that was okay too. We would be long gone by then. Keeping him in the dark about my mom being back was tough, and it made my disappearing acts even more confusing.

"Pull that map from the backseat." Mom interrupted my thoughts. We were on day three of our adventure.

Reaching over her shoulder, I pulled a large map with colored squiggly lines. "You know how to read this thing?" I crinkled my nose.

"Of course, girl! Big Ez showed me just what to do." Her eye darted between the map and the road. "You look at this thing! I'm over here trying to drive, girl. Just tell me where I can find I-10 and I'll get us there." She danced in her seat to no music.

A few hours later, Mom and I parked at a barbeque joint in Fort Worth, Texas. It was an old western style cattle ranch, and the servers strutted in cowboy hats and boots.

"This shit is good, girl!" Mom licked sauce from her fingers and palms. Her wig was sideways on her head and a speck of red barbecue sauce sat in her hair.

I snickered and eyed my plate of brisket, chicken, corn on the cob, beans, and cornbread.

"Ahh!" Mom shouted and jumped. The entire table shook under her legs, while gun shots rang out around us.

My eyes were wide as I adjusted to what was happening.

In a flash, the servers were running around the restaurant, shooting fake guns and challenging each other to duels. I gazed around at the other patrons; all looking embarrassed and nervous.

"Would anyone like to challenge Texas Pete to an old-fashioned shootout?" The server peeped around the restaurant.

"I will!" Mom stood up without a second thought.

I leaned back in my chair and watched my mom with her wig on lean and barbeque sauce in her hair, prance to the front of the room where she grabbed a fake gun.

"What's your name, little lady?" The announcer asked. He was at least 7 feet tall, and his cowboy hat was larger than the rest.

"You can call me Sonia. I am an entertainer myself," she said with a smug grin.

I smirked. She was never humble about anything.

"Well, you can call me Texas Pete, Ms. Sonia, and this here is the Battle of the Alamo, or we like to pretend that it is. You are battling our very own Bill Pickett, and he's a legend around these parts. Do you know how to duel?" He handed the microphone to Mom.

"Do I know how to duel? Why, of course I do. I'm from a small town called Tunica Rivers in Louisiana and we can do a little bit of everything! Ain't that right, my dear daughter?" Mom shouted at me in her English voice into the mic. She motioned for me to come to her.

I gulped my soda and pushed my seat back from the round dinner table as our table mates grinned in my direction. I scurried to stand by her side—embarrassed and excited.

"Oh, we've got ourselves a firecracker here!" He roused the crowd. They murmured and laughed. Texas Pete bowed at Mom and took backward steps.

"Mom, where should I stand?" I whispered. My shoulders bumping hers.

"Dear daughter, stand back as I give these amateurs a real show." Mom glared in Bill Pickett's direction. I must've blinked too soon or Mom had some Jedi mind tricks because in milliseconds, she was doing some sort of fancy footwork in front of the crowd. She hopped and skipped around, gyrating in weird motions while twirling the fake gun.

The crowd loved it.

She took a cowboy hat off a man sitting at the first table up front and flipped it onto her head.

I stood back and watched my mom, the original fly girl. My face was wide, and I was showing all my teeth grinning at her, but I didn't care. I didn't care. This woman was gold.

Mom grabbed my hands and said, "1, and 2 . . ." as she showed me her footwork.

"Mom! What is this?" I giggled, trying to match her steps. My cheeks were burning from smiling so hard, but I couldn't help it. This lady was crazy, but today it was the good kind.

"Just dance with me, my girl, dance with me." She moved around the room, pulling random people up with her until half the room was following behind Mom while she taught them her moves. Bill Pickett and Texas Pete looked at each other and shook their heads. They lost control of the room, but they didn't seem to mind. Mom was performing.

"All right, all right! We have to duel!" Mom said, straightening her face and back. She was at the center of the room with people forming a circle around her. She squared off with Bill Pickett and she took large steps backwards.

I held my breath. It was fake, but Mom was so good. So good and made it look so real.

Bill's jaw hardened as he reached for his waist, and soon, Mom shot her fake gun and the barrel popped like a firecracker. A red dart landed in the center of Bill Pickett's pants.

The crowd gasped while he fell to the floor, writhing in pain. "You couldn't aim for the chest? You're crazy, lady!" He cupped his pants. His face was contorted into a mean grimace, and he looked like he was about to cry.

Mom went and stood over top of him. "I told you where I come from, we know how to put on a show. And I'm not crazy. Right, Indy?"

"Right, Mom." I stared down at Bill as the crowd cheered behind us. "Right."

CHAPTER TWENTY-EIGHT

DAY FOUR

MOM AND I whizzed into Oklahoma. I felt funny not checking my phone, but I knew what would be there when I did. Text after text. Message after message. I picked at my nails while we zoomed down the highway. Taking our tour of the south, we touched down in Texas, New Mexico, and now Oklahoma in the matter of days. Mom didn't like to stay still for too long for fear that they were looking for us.

The car veered off to the right and when I gazed up; we were sideswiping a road sign. "Mom, watch out!" I screeched.

"Wha-what?" She stiffened. Her head jutted forward, and her eyes were huge while she jerked the car in the opposite direction.

I gripped my hands together as the car slammed to a stop. When I jumped out, cars whooshed by us so fast that the wind almost knocked me back.

"I just fell asleep a little, that's all!" Mom's English voice snapped. "Calm your nerves, girl. You always worry about the wrong things." She slammed on the back of the trunk and walked to the passenger side.

"What are you doing?" I frowned. My heart was beating in my temples.

"It's your turn to drive. Can't you see I'm tired!"

I checked out the damage and cringed at the deep scratch in the car running from the back to the front of The Bus.

Hopping into the driver's seat, I tilted my head and stared at Mom while she turned her back to me and snuggled under a blanket.

Hours later, my stomach settled and growled for food. I turned off at the nearest exit and found a small diner. Mom was lightly snoring next to me, and I wanted to slap her in the face and kiss her at the same time.

"What's that smell?" She croaked out from under her blanket. She wore my large, black sunglasses and looked every bit the troublemaker.

"Lunch. We need some food in us."

"Do we have lunch money?"

"We do."

"Then let's roll." Mom fluffed her breasts in her bra and straightened her wig. Her English accent was fluent now, and she was in full character.

Mom and I dined over omelets and pancakes, with her wolfing them down and me watching her in amazement. The woman could pack away food.

I pushed fried potatoes around on my plate and bit some of the cold, runny eggs. The food wasn't bad, but I usually had breakfast dates with Chaquille. And I missed Chaquille. He didn't understand why I needed to do this, and I really didn't either. I would never turn down time with my mom, though. When I glanced outside and recalled Mom side swiping the guard rail, I missed him even more.

"Mom. Can I have my phone?" I drawled. My eyes heavy and tired.

She wiped her mouth. "My dear daughter. I cannot give you your technological device at this time. We are on the run, my love."

"Well, how is this supposed to end?" I sighed. Maybe it was because it was time for Aunt Flo. Maybe it was because Mom and the road sign almost took us out back there. Or maybe it was because as days went on, I felt more guilty about lying to Dad. I mean, he needed me at home to help with Paisley and getting the new properties together. And here I was, traipsing around with Mom like some black ass Thelma and Louise. And the scary part was, that was actually kind of accurate.

"Look! Look over there!"

I strained my neck and squinted. In the distance, I made out a small building that said, *Psychic Readings Here.*

"C'mon dear daughter." She tugged at my arm. "Let's go!"

I threw a twenty-dollar bill on the table to cover the bill—the last I had.

"What the hell?" The waitress threw her hands up while we rushed by her.

"Sorry!" Mom shouted. She pulled me across the two-lane highway and cars beeped at us. When we made it across, we were breathless and sweating.

"Mom." I huffed. "What is this place?"

"Oh hush. Trust me for once." She flared her nostrils.

"If this cost money, I don't have anymore." I admitted.

"Don't worry, I've got this one." She straightened her outfit and hair once more before pushing the shop door open.

My chest rose. What money did she have? She watched me pay for everything the past three days and now she had money?

I entered the shop behind Mom, and an earthy smell tickled my nose.

"Ohh, this is fun, Indy."

"Don't be messing with them spirits."

"That girl will follow her Mama all the way to hell." One laughed.

The voices came in loud and clear as I tapped my foot.

"Welcome," a deep voice said from the back of the shop.

It was dark and I couldn't see through the haze sitting around my head and the low lighting. There were different crystals and trinkets hanging from the wall and plants. The plants were everywhere—winding up the spiral staircase, hanging from the ceiling, sprouting up like swords from big pots on the floor.

"Can I help you?" the deep voice repeated.

"Yes, we'd like tarot card readings?" Mom leaned over the counter; her breasts touched the glass.

"Are you both sure that's what you want?" the deep voice said. The shadow stepped forward, and an older woman with long black hair and a muu-muu dress stared back at us.

"Yes, we are sure," Mom said without looking my way.

"Fine. That will be $50.00," the woman with the deep voice said.

Mom reached into her bra and fished out a wad of damp money. She peeled it back, one bill at a time. "Here you go." She handed money to the woman.

The woman snatched it from Mom's hands almost as soon as she gave it to her. "You first." She pointed at Mom.

"I was going first anyway, my dear."

"And drop the accent." The woman scowled and plopped down into a chair across from Mom at a small table. I stood off to the side, watching everything.

"Are you a fire sign?" she questioned. She placed her hands over an open flame and waved it around like she was flicking something away.

"I am a Leo." Mom smiled.

"You're a performer."

"I would like to think so." Mom grinned and looked at me.

I crossed my arms and stood in the doorway.

"You have too many thoughts. All over the place. No direction."

Mom's smile disappeared.

"Lots of talent. On stage. As fast as the money rolls in, it rolls out..." she paused. The candle flame flickered in her pupil.

"People want to control you. Like a caged animal."

"Fuck them!" Mom exclaimed. She shifted in her seat and crossed her legs.

I listened to the woman's tone, and each sentence cut me. Mom didn't seem to find the seriousness of her words, but I did. I heard them all. My pocket burned from where my real cell phone used to sit, and I knew I had to find it.

"Your turn." The woman pointed to me.

I gulped. Shuffling towards the woman, Mom and I switched seats. "Isn't this great, my dear?" she whispered in her English voice so the woman didn't hear her.

I said nothing.

The woman shuffled a deck of cards and placed her hands over top of them and waited. She took a couple of deep breaths.

"You're a fire sign, too. But you act like a water sign. You feel things deeply."

I said nothing.

She pulled a few cards, and she frowned. "Death follows you. You're addicted to it."

"Dear heavens. She don't know the half of it! My Indy ain't to be fucked with!" Mom chuckled.

I squeezed my ankles together and clutched the table. I said nothing.

The woman shuffled the cards again and said, "Many people walk with you. Many ancestors, and many spirits. They pull you in different directions."

I gasped. Tears unleashed from my eyes and my chest heaved.

I said nothing.

"It has to be you. To end things," she whispered. Her dark skin and moles stared back at me.

"Dang, Indy. You had a good reading!" Mom squeezed my shoulder.

Grabbing tissues on the table, I rushed to wipe my eyes.

"That is time," the woman said and pushed back from the table and stood.

"This was fun! What did you say your name was, Miss Cleo?" Mom joked.

The woman looked Mom up and down and this time; she said nothing and walked to the back of the shop.

"Talk amongst yourselves!" Mom skipped out of the shop and shouted over her shoulder.

I wiped my eyes. "Talk to who, Mom?"

"The voices. They're all in there! I know you felt them too." She beamed.

I did feel them.

The long ride to the nearest motel felt even longer. The woman was right. It would be me to end things, but how? Mom went through so much to get to me, and the time that we spent together was probably the only time we would see each other like this. And Dad. Dad would be so disappointed in me. What would he say? My hands gripped the wheel. We had little money, but apparently, Mom had more. She tossed me another fifty dollars and said, "get us a room!" Before dozing off again. I had class, Synergy House, Paisley, Dad, Chaquille. Shit Will. I even had Will. I couldn't be this person with my mom. This person on the lam. This was the middle of my second year at Titus University and although I hadn't killed anyone, I tried.

JANAY HARDEN

I gazed over at Mom, asleep next to me. She took off her bra somewhere back on the highway and her titties were hanging down to her waist. On the floor, I saw money she kept tucked into her bra and the gleam of my phone. My real phone, not the burners we bought. She took it when we first got on the road.

Reaching down, I carefully pulled it toward me and eyed the road at the same time. "Humph!" I reached, and the car swerved into another lane. When I had the phone in my hand, I tucked it away in my own bra.

I had to call Chaquille.

CHAPTER TWENTY-NINE

I **SAT ON THE** bed and raised my eyebrows at her.

"Huh?" I squinted.

"Just do it, Indy!"

Mom lay sprawled on the bed, her shirt lifted over her head. She winced in pain. "I was scratching all night long. It was bothering me!"

"And what am I supposed to do?" I stared at the red and swollen boil my mom wanted me to pop up under one of her large breasts. "How did that even get there? I'm not popping that thing!" I shook my head and backed away.

"Oh girl, c'mon! I'll give you ten dollars. Mama Jackie used to make me and Ez pop hers when I was a kid and I hated it, too. But she made me do hers for free! At least you'll make a few bucks." Mom tilted her head and gave a dirty look.

The red eyed monster was round and filled with something that looked disgusting. Probably cottage cheese.

"How did that get there?"

"I used to get them a lot in Trochesse. I think it's the medicine they gave us. Shoot us up with different chemicals. It *has* to do something to our bodies. They got you on those meds

too, right? You'll see." Mom snickered. "I also think it's stress. That's when they really come up—when I'm stressed. You got me stressing, girl."

I shook my head in disgust. "This will never happen to me."

"Yeah, yeah. You'll see. Just squeeze it so the pus will come out. Please, Indy! Help your mom out! It itches something terrible!" She begged and threw herself back onto the bed.

Every bone in my body tensed as I leaned in closer with a wad of toilet paper in my hand. I turned away as my chilly fingers made contact with the red eyed monster.

"Okay. Okay." Mom inhaled a deep breath. "Squeeze!"

I shut my eyes and pinched the red eyed monster.

Seconds later, Mom yelped, and I felt hot liquid on the side of my face. "Ahhh!" I shouted. "It squirted on me!" I paddled to the bathroom, slammed the door shut behind me. I snatched a washcloth from the wall and scrubbed my face from where pus had assaulted me.

"Oh, oh, Indy. Thank you, girl. That feels so much better." Mom panted. "Now come and cut my hair so Minko and them won't know it's me." She was relieved, and I was almost blinded by tittie juice and love. Love blinded me.

After I chopped down Mom's hair with scissors she lifted from the dollar store, I stared at myself in the mirror. I turned my head from side to side and studied my skin. There were round bags under my eyes. I pulled at my cheeks and felt my dry, fat face. I sat on the toilet, but I didn't need to use it. My stomach knotted and twisted with each passing day with Mom, but my body wouldn't let me poop. Mom's stress made boils on her body. My stress had me wincing in pain, while my belly shot out lethal constipation cramps.

I closed my eyes, took a deep, breath and pulled my cell phone from my bra. Hiding it from Mom was easy and I don't even think she knew it was missing the way she carried on and sang

and danced for people. She didn't seem worried about being found out until she did, then she became a paranoid, crazy lady.

I pressed in the numbers I knew by heart. The number that I would never forget, no matter how many phones and gadgets and things that helped me forget it.

"Indy," He said..

"Will." The tears welled up in my eyes with one syllable.

"Where are you? Are you okay? Your Dad came by here asking if I've seen you. You know, he went to the police and told them you were missing. He tried to make them look for you, but they said you were an adult and you probably ran off on your own." Will shot out words, but my voice was caught in my throat like The Little Mermaid.

Dad was looking for me and had called the police. I wonder if he told them about Mom.

"I-I I'm okay. We're okay." I croaked.

"We?"

"My mom. I'm with my mom."

Will breathed into the phone.

"Indy. . . oh, Indy." He whispered.

I covered my hands with my mouth as the hot tears spilled over my fingers. "We'll be home soon." I spat out. "Please don't tell my dad that you talked to me. I. . . I. . . I just needed to hear your voice."

"Do the right thing, Indy. Do the right thing. I love you."

"I love you too." I croaked.

"What are you doing in there, girl! Let's go! I'm trying to go see this Will Smith movie. You know I met him once? He came to one of *The FatCats* shows in Tallahassee. I said to him after the show, you want to come see what else I *will* do?" Mom cracked up, and I heard her slap her leg.

I quickly flushed the toilet and wiped my face. I stared at myself once more before shutting off the light.

"What were you in there doing? What took so long? Don't no dookie take that long?" Mom eyed me.

"I was talking to myself." I assured. I grabbed the keys to The Bus and locked the motel door behind us.

"I be talking to myself too, not crying, girl. When you talk to yourself, you don't be crying. That is how you get what you want. You imagine it and believe it. You don't cry about it."

With a sigh, I backed out of the parking space and hopped onto the highway. I didn't know what she was talking about.

"What do you think about just leaving that itty bitty school of yours and us moving to Seattle?"

"Seattle?

Mom leaned in close with a sly grin. "Yeah, Seattle. That's way across the country! We can get a little cabin and I can make another band, and if anyone messes with us. Well, we can take them out! Together! All we have to do is get Sidney. She probably won't want to go, but we know what's best for her, right?" Mom winked and switched into her English voice and talked so fast, I could barely keep up with her.

"I want to stay in school. I am staying in school." I asserted. Not knowing what she would say, I paused as each word came out. "And Sidney is staying at home. She is not a part of this."

"Fine! When you decide to really love yourself, you'll call me! Pull over! Let me drive, girl." Mom instructed.

When we switched, she adjusted the seat and roared down the road. My head slammed against the seat.

"Slow down. You don't have to go so fast."

"Mind your business. If you would've just popped the thing when I told you to pop it, we wouldn't be running late for Mr. Smith and his fine self." She erupted. Her eyes looked crazed and dark. "Indy! How about we go for fifty points today? Want to take someone out?" Her eyes widened.

"No, Mom. . . I want to go back to school. This was fun. . . but I have to go back."

"Indy, college will always be there. And you know these people are trying to take me away. Is that what you want to happen? Do you want to see me locked up like some animal? I can't believe you would choose college over me. Well, I should've known. You are your daddy's child."

"What's wrong with Daddy?" I sat up in the seat and glared. My dad was the best there was and when she went and got herself locked away, he picked up the pieces for me and Sidney. She was taking things too far now.

"Nothing is wrong with him! I just think ya'll give up too easy. You need the fire spirit, Indy! The fire!" She giggled.

I stared at her in disbelief as she talked so fast her head was shaking. I had been wrong—so wrong.

My mom was sick. Just like everyone had said, but I refused to believe it. She came in like a hurricane and took everything in her wake, and I followed her blindly. She wanted to uproot Sidney's life and change who she was as a person. She wanted me and Sidney to be some sort of teenage, outlawed bandits. She didn't care about our futures—she simply wanted to get even with men and have fun while doing it. She loved us but not for who we were, but for who she re-imagined us to be. I reimagined her too, and she wasn't the person I made her out to be in my head.

I had to turn Mom in and break this chain.

I was carrying around drama that wasn't even mine to carry—but I did. For her. A lump formed in my throat as I watched my mom go on and on about everything and nothing. My right hand gripped the door handle as she zoomed down the roadway, speeding.

The weight of Mom was too much to carry, and I had to let her go. Had to. I squinted, trying not to cry. "Mom. . . I think. . . we should. . ." and before I could get the words out, my head slammed against the window as we side-swiped another guard rail and The Bus hummed to a stop.

"Are you ladies okay?" I heard a voice ask.

Everything was blurry. Everything sounded like I was under water.

"Wha-What?" I groaned. My side was hurting something terrible. Mom! Where was Mom? I adjusted my eyes to the darkness and realized Mom and I were laying on our sides, hanging out of The Bus. Every window was shattered and the voice that asked if we were okay sounded so far away, but I knew he was close. In the distance, I heard the wail of the ambulance moving closer to us. I looked over at Mom. She lay motionless, suspended in the car with a long trickle of fresh blood over her eye and saturating her hair.

"Mom. . . Mom." I nudged her. She didn't budge.

"Try not to move her!" the voice shouted. "We have to wait until the ambulance arrives."

I tried to stay as still as I could, but a searing pain whipped through my side again. "Please, call my Dad. Benjamin. Benjamin Barre from Tunica Rivers." I croaked.

And then I saw black.

CHAPTER THIRTY

"**N**O REALLY, I am fine," I said, pushing the stetho-scope from my chest. The hospital people wanted to poke and prod me every few minutes. Besides bruising to my rib cage, I made it out of the car accident with few scrapes. "Did someone call my dad?" I eyed the team of doctors huddled in a corner, deciding what to do about me.

"Yes, we did, Ms. Lewis. He took the first available flight and should be here any minute."

"And my mom?" I dropped my shoulders.

"She is. . . a character. She has a nasty cut on her forehead that required a few stitches, but otherwise, she is okay. She is asking to see you but given her. . . uh mental state. We wanted to wait for your father to arrive. Ms. Lewis. We also called the police. They are on their way."

"And why did you do that?" I mustered up the strength to screech. My side ached like a bitch. I was relieved. Sad. Happy it was over. Shocked.

"Well, when you first came in you were delirious. We had to give you something to calm you down. You were screaming about fire and water. You said your mom was on the run. We

thought it best to call the police and when we did, they said she was a missing person and not to leave her alone."

I breathed a sigh of relief. Mom was okay and Dad was on the way. So were the police.

It was over.

I wanted to go home and then to school. I didn't want to be on the run with Mom. The past few days were fun until they weren't. Until we were both laid up in hospital beds.

Nurses buzzed around the emergency room in a flurry of Crocs and scrubs, everyone's adrenaline rushing. My room was white. So white and I can't believe some crazy person decided hospitals should be this bleak and bare. My side was still hurting and aching, but nothing was hurting more than my heart.

"Did anyone find my purse?" I asked one nurse.

"Sure thing." She gave me a sad smile and handed it to me. When I opened it, the sharp pains returned to my chest while I gritted my teeth. Searching through my bag, I found what I was looking for.

Minko Forrest.

I palmed the phone number and name on the card, just like I had done days earlier. Only now, I knew what had to be done. I pressed the area code into my cell phone.

"Indy?"

The card and my purse dropped from my hand and the tears fell like rain.

"Dad!" I cried.

He scurried to me and grabbed me so hard, the wind left me. "Are you okay? Let me look at you! What are you doing in Oklahoma? Where is your mom? Don't answer any of that. Are you okay?"

"Dad. . . I'm so sorry." I choked out through snot. "I just wanted to be with her again. Like old times. And the car. Ez's car. Dad, I'm so sorry." I wailed.

Dad looked around at the attendants in the room watching the show and nodded. They exited the room, leaving us alone with the beeps of a busy hospital.

"Indy, don't you worry about The Bus. You are safe. You are safe! I was worried sick. I knew this had something to do with your mom. No parent wants a late-night phone call from the police asking for the parent of Indigo Lewis. That just about broke my heart." Dad paused and for the first time since Ez passed, I saw tears in his eyes. "I don't know what I would do if I lost you. You're my firstborn. You're my oldest child. I need you here with me. You have to let someone in Indy, you have to!" The tears fell from Dad's eyes, and he didn't wipe them away. He held onto me so tight I didn't know if I had chest pains from him or from the actual pain.

I cried into my dad's arms for what seemed like forever. The hospital whirled around us and when my sobs died down and my chest pains settled, I looked up into my dad's face and told him. About the voices. Trying to get a therapist and the fiasco that's been. I told him about the medication, and about school being hard. I hesitated when I told him when Mom first showed up at Synergy House. I even told him I thought I was dying because of my chest pains and all. I told him how ugly I felt with my hair chopped off. I talked and talked until my throat was raw. I didn't tell him about Jaxon, Mr. Chestnut, or what's-his-name. When I was done talking, my body felt lighter and the pain in my chest faded like a faint drum.

"Indy. Your chest pains are probably anxiety. You know your Mama Jackie used to have terrible anxiety. She used to call it catching the rapture. Why do you think she spent so much time at home going nowhere? She said people and large crowds made her catch the rapture."

Sitting up on my back elbows, my mouth fell open. "You mean I'm not dying?"

"I don't think so. But we're in the right place to find out." Dad patted my hand.

"These voices of yours..." Dad paused. "Have you hurt yourself? Or anyone else?"

I looked my dad in the eye. The words were on the tip of my tongue, ready to spill any second now. I could taste them lingering in my mouth, wanting to be spit out. I swallowed them away. "No Dad. But they make it hard to concentrate on anything else." I lied.

A glimmer of ease washed over his face, and I was relieved that he was relieved.

"Dad. Look on the floor, under my bed. Grab my purse for me."

Dad rummaged under the bed and handed me my purse and some of the contents that had fallen on the floor.

I fingered the card I was looking out before Dad walked in. Minko Forrest.

"Dad. . . I think we should call him," I said through red and blurry eyes.

Dad sighed, and his eyes were red and blurry too. "I already did, Indy. He's on his way."

"Can I see her one last time?" I sniffled. This was too much. I had my mom and then lost her again in a matter of weeks.

"I don't see why not. I want to see her too." Dad admitted. "You know I love your mom, Indy. I always have. But I think it's high time we all accept that she is sick, and she's not the same Mom that we remember. We have to love her from afar, honey. Wherever that is. Whether it's Trochesse, New York, or somewhere else. We have to keep fighting. We have to move forward. With Ez too. Ez lives on in all of us, and we need to honor his life by moving forward."

I worried so much about the thoughts in my head and keeping Mom's secrets from everyone that I failed to realize just how much Dad still loved Mom. The guilt settled even more into my stomach and I felt sick.

"Like moving forward with the houses." I swallowed the saliva growing in my mouth.

"Yes, like with the houses." Dad gave a half-smile. "Ez would be so proud of us. He probably already is. He's going to watch over our land and our houses, make sure we are prosperous from the other side. He's stronger on the other side, Indy! I got a call from some man the other day, he wants to interview me soon about the property close to your school. Affordable housing for college students, he said. Can you believe it? Us, landlords?" Dad chuckled.

I cocked my head back and checked out my dad—the landlord, carpenter, the new father, the man of the house to Ms. Arletha, the hood philosopher. He was everything. "Us, landlords!" I smiled.

"Uh, family? Ms. Sonia Lewis is requesting your presence in her room?" A tall doctor interrupted us. I hobbled out of the bed when I heard a commotion in the hallway. Dad and I shot a glance at each other, knowing that Mom was somewhere putting on a show.

We shuffled into the hallway and saw Mom darting between doctors and Minko Forrest.

"Please, Ms. Lewis. Let's not do this the hard way. We will take you into custody tonight and returned to Trochesse. Let your family say their goodbyes." Minko pressed against the wall and gave Mom space.

A nurse sitting in the center pod had her hand on a small panic button under her desk and she looked like she was itching to press the button.

"Do you know who I am? I am Sonia Lewis. Mother to Indigo and Sidney. Daughter to Ezra and Jackie..." Mom started in her English voice. A small crowd formed around her, but this time

it wasn't her adoring admirers smiling; it was doctors and the hospital police. Mom gazed around at the sea of white coats, white walls, and white people before her eyes landed on me and Dad. Her eyes softened as she looked between us. The double doors divided us, and staff members were tugging at her arms, trying to take her to a back room.

"We almost had it all, didn't we, Ben?" Mom batted her eyes. She snatched off her wig that was already sitting sideways and exposed her short auburn hair. Dad held my hand and squeezed it when he did that.

"Indy. Choose yourself, my girl. Choose yourself!" Mom shouted down the hallway.

I squeezed Dad's hand back.

"Okay." I mouthed to Mom, and I meant it. I would choose myself and I wouldn't worry about the wrong things anymore. Mom had to go.

"Enough, Ms. Lewis. Please turn around." Minko Forrest interrupted. He was shorter than Mom and probably the worst private detective in the history of private detectives.

Mom gaped at me and Dad, standing shoulder to shoulder. So many people, memories, and history stood between us. Things that couldn't be erased, not by fire, water, or tittie boils.

"See you guys soon." Mom mouthed and blew a kiss. She turned around as Minko Forrest read her Miranda Rights and placed cuffs on her wrists.

PART III
REDEMPTION

CHAPTER THIRTY-ONE

I **LOOKED UP AT** the house. They painted it a light shade of blue, flowers were planted, and the grass was cut too low. Dad could build a house, but Lord knows he would tear up some grass if someone let him. I chuckled to myself.

"You guys are here! Finally, we were waiting forever for you." Dad lumbered out the house with a big, sheepish grin. He shook hands with Chaquille, who was also giddy as he looked around at the house that they worked so hard on.

"Shall we give you the grand tour, Indy?" Sidney said, hiding behind Dad. Paisley cooed in her arms and I ran to her, almost tripping up the front step.

"Paisley!" I screamed and outstretched my arms.

Sidney grinned and handed me my baby sister, the youngest in charge.

"Isn't she growing like a weed, Indy?" Ms. Arletha beamed.

She was, she sure was. Paisley was round and little baby rolls of fat kept her plump. Her skin was surely Hershey kissed, and she reminded me of an adorable, chocolate version of the Michelin Man.

"Hi Miss Paisley." I snuggled close to her and smelled her. Why did babies smell so damn good? Closing my eyes, I sniffed her again.

It was weeks since they took Mom back to Trochesse with a transfer to New York State Home for the Criminally Insane in the works. I assumed they had her padlocked somewhere they could easily monitor her. As much as I tried not to focus on Mom or what she was doing, dreams of her came every night.

Yesterday I was laying in bed with Chaquille and he pulled a few kernels from under the pillow. *"What the heck is this?"* He held up the hardened popcorn. I started to explain that Mom would eat in bed when she was hiding out, but then I would have to explain a lot of things and I didn't have the energy.

Real life was here and in front of me, and I couldn't look back anymore. Paisley was proof of that and I would have been crazy to miss these moments.

I took in the front foyer of the home. Dad and Chaquille worked on the property closest to Titus University. It was only about forty minutes from me and about one hour from Dad in the opposite direction. We both could easily get to the home if there were any issues. Chaquille was taking the daily responsibilities now that his physical therapy had ended. He was on a better cocktail of medications to help curb his seizures, and he talked less and less about dropping out of college and more about renting and flipping houses. It was funny. Ez's death allowed us to purchase two homes to renovate and rent out. Dad wanted a third but Ms. Arletha told him to pace himself and see how the first two went. The homes energized Dad and gave him something to do with his grief, and it inspired Chaquille to figure out what he wanted to do with his life.

Life was really wild.

"So, Indy. This is your first time seeing everything since we finished. What do you think?" Chaquille asked. He had a smirk on his face. The house was nice and he knew it.

"You guys did a great job!" I looked around and took in everything. The home was white. Not white like the hospital, but white like everything was clean and new. They even had it staged with some furniture pieces, so it would look more homey.

"We didn't use high-end anything. We used laminate counters and floors, but I don't think you can even tell the difference. Go ahead, get close to it, Indy. See? You can't even tell!" Dad beamed. He was so proud of himself, and my heart swelled with pride. In Ez's demise, Dad found his way. He was excited about the future, and that was something I'd never witnessed. Spending years hunched over toilets and fixing old radiators, his true talents could shine through, and shining he was.

"Dad, it's gorgeous." I breathed.

"Chaquille did most of the flooring, and I handled the cabinets and bathroom. The only thing we have left is to rip up the carpets in the bedrooms. I want to do one last walk through and make sure we don't see any mold in the bathrooms or water damage around the perimeter. There was some before and I watched a YouTube video about how to clean it up. But otherwise—"

"It's perfect." I cut in. "Otherwise, it's perfect." I finished for him.

Dad leaned against the freshly painted wall and smiled.

"I bought some pots and pans for the kids when they move in." Ms. Arletha shuffled throughout the kitchen, breaking down boxes to throw away.

"I told her not to, but she insisted." Dad rolled his eyes.

"Of course, honeydew. If we rent to college students, they don't know nothing about getting no proper cooking pans. Everyone should have a nice baking dish. It's just luxury." Ms. Arletha countered.

I understood it so clearly at this moment. Dad did all of this for us. For me—for Sidney, Paisley, and Ms. Arletha. Mom insinuated Dad was weak, and Ez made fun and thought of him as a pushover. He was none of those things. He worked hard to take care of the ladies in his life, and as I looked around with tears in my eyes, he used his bare hands to do it.

"Come in the backyard with me, Indy," Dad said.

I followed him to the back patio where we walked around the house looking for any pooling water lines. In Louisiana, water damage meant future problems, especially the way hurricanes loved to set up shop on the Gulf Coast.

"We'll have to look at that spot over there." I pointed to a dark mark on the side of the house.

Dad scribbled the location on a clipboard and took a picture with his cellphone.

"How is counseling going? And the medication?" Dad tucked the clipboard under his arm and glanced at me.

I sighed. I had sessions with Ms. Ramos twice a week now. Trenita returned from medical leave in another month, and although I missed her, me and Ms. Ramos, and her crazy eye, somehow bonded. Dad called The Wellness Center and spoke to the lead clinical therapist. I'm not sure what he said, but soon after we left the hospital, Ms. Ramos was calling to schedule double weekly sessions and she was consulting with the Titus University psychiatrist for a medication change. I was honest with her. I told her I stopped taking them because they made me tired and I slept through my classes. Ms. Ramos jajaja'ed and said, *"That's all? There are many medications, Indy. We could have tried something else!"*

The psychiatrist prescribed me an anti-psychotic medication. I cringed when he said the words and I repeated it in my mind. It didn't sound like me or anything that I wanted to attach myself to—but if it would help the voices, I would

try it. The voices were far and few between these days and I was grateful.

"It's going good, Dad." I shifted out of my thoughts. "I think it's helping. Some."

"And have you met with the academic counselor? Any more word on your academic probation?"

I smiled. In this entire fiasco that was my life, school was the one thing that had worked out well while I was on the lam with Mom. "We were close to midterms anyway when. . . when Mom and I left. So most of my professors let me make up the tests. After I explained what happened, of course. Only one of my professors didn't want to hear it and gave me a zero for the time missed. I'll have to make up that class sometime next year."

"And how do you feel about that?" Dad asked.

We stopped walking, and he stared at me like he was trying to read my thoughts. This is the part I hated. Dad knew most of my deepest worries, and it made him worry. Most of his questions these days consisted of words like *feel, think, and mood.* I turned him into a pseudo therapist the way he questioned me about my thoughts.

"I don't really feel any way about it. I mean, Mom and I left. This is me taking accountability for what I've done," I said, digging my shoes into the wet ground and kicked at a rock in the yard.

"And Synergy House? What have they said?"

"Mr. John said I accumulated some sick days. He actually was pretty understanding about it once I explained about Mom . . ."

And he was. I placed so much disdain surrounding him and Bryce that maybe I never gave him a fair shake. He said, *"my older sister suffered from mental health issues. I saw some wild things growing up with her. Writing became my outlet when things got*

to be too much. Maybe that's why you like to write too." I held my head a little higher after my conversation with Mr. John. He let me keep my job and gave me something to think about. I lost myself in words and the literary musings of others. They were the voices in my head long before the real ones came along. Even though my writing got away from me in college, Mr. John's compassion reminded me of my love for the craft. I vowed right then and there to get out of my own way and return to my imagination filled with random nouns, verbs, and words that spoke to me. On the paper, not in my head.

And Bryce.

Even thinking his name made my jaw clench. After I sat and thought about the computer fiasco, I really had no proof that he off'ed my article. That was another battle I had to let go. We only had a few more months of working together, and I needed to get used to working with people in the real world without wanting to hurt them. It was a work in progress but with the meds, it didn't seem like such a daunting task. I was glad that he didn't die that night at Driskill Mountains.

I was finding my way too. And it felt right.

On the ride back home, Chaquille rested his eyes on me blinking out the window. "Anything on your mind?"

"So many things." I murmured.

"Indy. Since we've been together, shit has gone down! You are one of the smartest people I know and you keep halfway flunking out of college. I became your neighborhood carpenter with the help of your dad. . ." He chuckled.

"And your seizure." I reminded.

"I didn't forget about that one."

We locked eyes.

"My point is. We've made it through. Life got real for us in a short amount of time, but we made it through. You have to start talking to me. You can't keep things bottled up like this. And you definitely can't harbor a fugitive in your room, again." He shot me a side-eye.

"Chaquille, I want to talk to you about something. . . Will—"

"Hold on, let me finish, woman. I love you. And whatever it is you're going through in that mind of yours. Let me be your lighthouse in the darkness." He glanced at me with nervous eyes. He grabbed then caressed my hand. Our fingers intertwined and he held them with a firm grip. "Now, what were you going to say?"

I gulped. Will. I wanted to tell him how I cried to Will the day I left him at my dad's house. And how he was still on my mind, even through all of this. I wanted to atone for my actions and hold myself accountable before karma did that for me. Too many cords and soul ties bound me to Will, and I wasn't sure if I could unpack them in one conversation with Chaquille. Instead, I licked my lips and nodded.

"I wanted to say I love you too, Chaquille."

CHAPTER THIRTY-TWO

"**I**NDY, YOU REALLY don't have to do that. I know things happen," Laylah Capri said.

I held the phone tighter to my ear and twirled the cord in my hand. "No, it's the least that I can do. I want to make this right. I felt terrible about losing the article. I talked to my supervisor, and he's allowing me to re-write the piece, and he'll even let me add a photo of us from our last meeting! If you are still interested, of course." I waited with bated breath for her response. Mr. John let me add graphics to the article and I believe it was because he felt bad about everything happening with my mom. He was checking in every few days now when we were in the office together and he insisted I texted him after hours if there were any issues.

There was a pause. "I know you feel like you messed up, but I am grateful to have you on the team, Indy. The way you dedicate yourself to things is admirable. Of course, BFN is still interested. Thank you."

I covered my mouth with a tempered smile, and I wondered if she felt me through the phone. I was sure Laylah could hear my grin. "I'll get started right away!" We hung up, and I spun

in my chair and did a little dance. I was thrilled! Disappointing Laylah and the *Black Feminists Nation* was not of my own doing—but I could still try to make it right.

For the next two hours, my focus was laser sharp. I typed and typed. Deleted, printed, highlighted, trashed, almost cried—and tried to remember as much of the previous article from memory as I could. With Chaquille in my room watching football and screaming at the tv, Synergy House after hours was the perfect place to get as much done as I could with minimal interruptions. I stopped writing and pressed the save icon at least a hundred times. Kathleen showed me how to play with Google drive and if I could help it, I would never lose another piece of writing.

"What are you doing here?" He demanded. He saw me here a few weeks ago so I didn't understand where all this spice in his words was coming from.

Spinning around in my seat, I looked Bryce up and down slowly, making sure he saw every bit of my contempt. "I'm working. Is there a problem?"

"No. I just thought I would be here alone." He hustled to his desk and flicked on his computer. His eyebrows were furrowed and face pinched.

I saved my work repeatedly. Although I was almost done, something wouldn't let me head home with him being there. The last time we worked together like this, my article disappeared.

I'd be damned if that happened again.

I browsed on the internet and played with my phone for a few minutes, but really I studied Bryce behind his computer. He was typing like a madman and really seemed to be in a groove of writing, thinking, and feverishly writing again. I wanted to go around to his computer and pull the power cord directly from the wall, so he knew what it felt like to lose it all.

"You got this, Indy. Calm yourself down. Don't let him get the best of you," A voice said.

My breathing was shallow and fast. I eyed his every keystroke. Grabbing a piece of gum and chewing for dear life, I tried to occupy my mind and mouth so I didn't cuss his ass out, or worse. The worst seemed to be my favorite, and some days, that was okay. Would today be an okay day?

"Go home, Indy. Go home," a voice said.

I held my breath and tried not to hyperventilate.

Change your energy, Indy. Get up, go somewhere, but change your energy. Anxiety will not win, I said to myself.

Ms. Ramos and I spent our last session discussing how to calm my body during an anxiety attack and now seemed like the perfect time since I wanted to reach across the table and attack.

With a deep exhale, I pressed save one last time and slowly logged out of each setting on the computer. I shut it down and waited until the screen was completely dark before I stood and grabbed my jacket behind my chair.

"Are you heading out?

"Yes, I'm going home."

"So sorry to hear about your mom. That's really crappy." Bryce stopped typing and leaned back in his chair. His stare was icy and didn't match the words that came out of his mouth.

"Yea, thanks." I mumbled, putting on my jacket.

Against my better judgement, the words tumbled out of my mouth. "Oh, and Bryce. I powered down everything on my computer. So, there's no mishaps. Like last time. Okay?"

Bryce's shoulders shook. I went to physical therapy with Chaquille, and they taught me what a seizure looked like. It always started in the shoulders and for one split second. I wondered if Bryce was having a seizure. The deep belly laugh that accompanied his shoulder shakes told me otherwise.

He was laughing at me.

"We're still talking about your article, huh?" He pushed away from his computer, crossed his arms behind his head, and leaned back. "Listen, Indy. I don't know what happened to your little black girl article. Even if I did, do you think I would sit here and tell on myself? I mean, when Harper was here, you had it made. She put your mediocre work on the front page. When I write about things that matter. Matter!" He slapped his chest and his face turned red. "My piece from Mr. John is going to blow people away. I've been working day and night to get it ready, and guess what? Mr. John is still giving you a leading article with graphics all because your mom is crazy and he feels bad. I'm glad your article disappeared. Maybe next time you'll be more careful about logging out and follow the rules like we're supposed to. Who doesn't know how to back up their work these days? You know these things happen. Oh, and Indy. I keep my Epi-Pen with me everywhere I go now. Everywhere. You know, just in case." His eyes turned dark at his last sentence.

"You call me Indigo." A low moan rattled from my chest, and I barreled around the table, itching for my fingers to be around Bryce's neck. He stood up from his chair and his jaw was tight. Bryce was taller than me, but not by much. He wasn't muscular, but he didn't look weak either. I knew he had something to do with my article disappearing; he basically admitted it! He also kind of admitted to knowing that I purposely poisoned him—and that would be hard for me to explain.

I was at an impasse.

We stood staring at each other, waiting for the other to break.

We glared up and down, no more words spoken. I saw him—I *really* saw him. He was jealous about my friendship with Harper and felt like people gave me chances because they felt bad for me.

Nepotism. He thought it was nepotism.

These were things I already knew but didn't have proof. Shit, I still didn't have proof technically, but his audacity tasted so vile that I didn't need proof of what I already knew.

With a low growl and the voices threatening to take him out right there, I sized him up. I wouldn't be able to take him in a man-to-man, or man-to-woman fight; but we would have our day. Someway, somehow—we would have our day.

I scurried out of Synergy House and leaned against the front door. I was grateful for the breeze. I closed my eyes and took in a sharp breath before breaking into a full sprint to my car. Or car rental, I should say. The Bus was no more and was undrivable after the accident with Mom. Dad rented me a small Kia Optima. It was shiny and new, but it didn't smell like Ez, like The Bus did.

I slammed my car door closed and put the keys into the ignition before I called Mr. John. The phone rang and rang before his voicemail picked up. It was almost 8.p.m. but he told me to call at any time. People stayed working in the office until at least midnight, so it wasn't *that* late. But still, it was just me and Bryce this night. I pressed end and didn't leave a message before I switched to my messages. I sent him a quick text.

> **ME:** Please call me when you get a chance. It's about my article.

I sped down the road and turned into Theodora's apartment complex since it was the closest to Synergy House. I had to talk to someone.

"Indy. Are you okay?" Theodora stared me up and down and clutched her sweater around her chest.

I pushed past her into the apartment, rambling.

"He did it! He all but admitted to it. I knew it! I knew it!" I fumed. My hands were shaking while I paced Theodora's white carpet.

"Hi, Indy." Dylan waved from the couch. He and Theodora shot looks back and forth at each other with worried expressions.

"Who did what, Indy?" Theodora pressed.

"Bryce! I know he did something to my article. He didn't say it exactly, but. . . but. . . I know it was him!" I traipsed back and forth, slapping my hands together.

"Indy. Let this go." Theodora breathed. She tilted her head and squinted.

I stared at her. "Excuse me?"

"Indy, Bryce is a nice guy. He was only trying to find out what happened to Mr. Chestnut, and you seem to have issue after issue with him, Indy. I'm your girl. You know I love you. But seriously. You have something against Bryce. Maybe it's time to let it go."

"Theodora. I just told you he deleted my article. He admitted to it!"

"What did he say, exactly?"

Dylan muted the tv and waited for my response. I was grateful because I could hear myself think.

"He said. . . he wouldn't tell on himself. He said. . . mediocre. He said . . ." I stammered.

He said nothing. Nothing that would prove anything. I could prove that he deleted my article just like he could prove that I poisoned him.

We both *saw* each other but once again—I looked like a crazy girl. I wanted to scream from sheer frustration.

"Indy. It's okay. It's okay. Indy." Theodora led me to the couch and held me as I cried.

I had so much information, but really—I had nothing. "I'm going to go. I'm okay."

Dylan gave a bewildered look, trying not to stare. "It's okay, Indy, you can stay for as long as you need."

Theodora ran her fingers through the back of my hair and I cringed—phantom memories of where my braids used to be.

"I'm fine. I'll text you when I get home." I reassured, but I was anything but reassured myself.

With a hand squeeze and a thoughtful gaze, Theodora walked me to my car and watched me pull off.

CHAPTER THIRTY-THREE

"**D**O SOMETHING FOR yourself, Indy. What makes you happy? Makes you feel good?" Ms. Ramos said during our session.

It was a beautiful day outside, but I was failing to see the beauty in anything right now. My mood was up and down. Back and forth. Some days I was on a high and feeling like I could take on the world, other days I wanted to curl into my bed. But at least now I was more aware of it. Ms. Ramos made me feel like we would figure it out together. What made me feel good? What made me happy?

A few hours later, I stared at myself in the mirror. I foamed mousse into my hands and pressed it over my freshly done braids. Opting for five cornrows going straight back, I adorned small gold pieces to the ends and checked out my face from side to side. Not bad, not bad at all. *Back like I never left,* I whispered.

I didn't ask Theodora to do my hair. We were in a weird space after I showed up to her apartment. There was a new shop in town close to campus and it wasn't how Theodora used to keep me laced, but it was damn good.

I slathered some gloss onto my lips when my phone rang. Chaquille was FaceTiming me.

"Hey Bae." I grinned.

"Look at you! Looking how you looking!" he whooped loudly.

My cheeks flushed as I giggled.

"You look amazing, woman! So beautiful. I forgot why I even called. Damn!"

He stared at me in the phone. I tried my best to play it cool, but my face was already hurting from cheesing so hard. When I cut my hair last year after Ez died, I was in a bad place. My braids had seen me through some tough times, and with the back of my neck constantly exposed, I *felt* exposed. These braids and I were a packaged deal, and when my hair was done, my mood was better. I changed my energy just like Ms. Ramos suggested.

"What can I help you with, Mr. Fox?" I batted my eyes.

"I finally remembered. You and that face had me dumb for a second. Anyway, the new tenant texted and asked to have the keys tomorrow so they could start moving things in. Do you mind running over there and putting the keys in the lockbox?"

"They're moving in early?"

"They asked your dad to move in a few things early and he said yes."

I smiled. My dad found his first tenants for the property closest to Titus. College students splitting the rent. Chaquille was managing the property, but he was in New York visiting his mom until this weekend. The house wasn't perfect and still needed a few things completed, but Dad was so excited that he listed it anyway. The college students didn't care, and before we knew it—a date was set, keys were cut, and they were moving in.

"Sure, I can take them over. Where are the keys?"

"Check in my gym bag under the bed."

I reached under the bed and pulled out his gym bag. It was full of neatly filed papers, all relating to the house, and a few sets of keys. "Wow, look at you, Mr. Property Manager!"

"I'm a business *mannn*." He gave a smug smile and rubbed his chin.

"I'll take them over today." I giggled. Chaquille was so crazy.

I blew him a kiss and hung up. I put Ez's dog tags around my neck and a gold bracelet on my wrist. My phone rang again and when I looked down, the name and face made me weak in the knees.

"Hey, Will." I breathed. He called.

"What are you doing?" he asked. His seatbelt was slapped across his chest and he was zooming down the road.

"About to head to one of Dad's properties in a few minutes. Where are you going? I didn't think you stepped foot out of Tunica Rivers."

Will chuckled. "We got jokes I see. Actually, I was in your neck of the woods. I had to come this way to take my plumber's certification exam."

"And?" I held my breath.

"I passed, Indy! I am officially a plumber!"

"Ahhh! Will, that is amazing! I'm so proud of you!" I shouted. Will studied the past two years for his certification while his family laughed at him for not making any money. He was official now, and about to be rolling in dough! "So, what can you do now? I'm sure Dad can use a plumber on the team! At least for the Tunica Rivers properties." Dad would surely hire Will in a second.

"Well, of course, the obvious. I can fix most plumbing issues, but I can also do some contracting work. I can be your maintenance man," Will said. I was checking everyone's energy these days and Will was giving crazy energy.

"Listen, since you're in the area. I have to stop by Dad's property close to Titus anyway to drop off keys. Do you want to meet me there and check it out?"

Will smiled. "Drop me the location. I'll be there shortly."

I hung up from Will and scrambled through the room, tossing on my shoes. I pressed perfume into my neck, wrists, and I pulled my tights from my waist and sprayed down there too.

CHAPTER THIRTY-FOUR

I **PUSHED THE KEYS** into the door and looked around before the house would be filled with rowdy college students. Chaquille said to leave the keys in the lockbox, but I peered around and checked out the house one last time while waiting for Will. It sat back away from the road, and it was almost private with trees and a fence lining the half-acre property. He was going to love this. My dad was a landlord, Will was a plumber, and Chaquille was a makeshift realtor. I chuckled at the irony of it all.

"Indy?" a confused voice asked.

Have you ever felt a chill all the way down to your spine? It's like, you're not really cold but at the same time, you know something bad is about to happen and your body senses it before you do?

Spinning around, the sight of him nauseated me.

Bryce.

"What are you doing here?" he asked. He stomped his foot and had a small notebook in hand.

"What am I doing here?" My eyes bugged out. "What are you doing here? This is my dad's place."

"What? That's not right." Bryce dug in his pocket but came up short. "Crap! I left my phone in the car. I have the owner as. . . hold on one second." Bryce flips through his notebook and I wanted to poke his eyes with his pen with each turn of his pages, filled with notes.

"Benjamin Barre," Bryce and I said at the same time.

"That's your father? I didn't recognize the name."

"Why are you here?" I demanded to know. Enough of the questions. Bryce was in my face. In my space. I needed to know why.

A smug grin spread across Bryce's face and he walked throughout the space, eyeing the newly renovated house. "This really is a small world." He puffed out his chest and I caught the gleam of a small diamond stud in his ear.

Jaxon used to wear diamond studs and puffed out his chest, like he was better than me.

Trembling under anger threatening to boil, I cleared my throat. "Why are you here?" I took a step back and looked behind me. Was there anything to grab just in case I needed to defend myself? *Did* I need to defend myself?

"Mr. John trusted me with a front-page story, and I intend to deliver. Regardless of who it's connected to. But this just works out perfectly." He beamed.

"What are you talking about, asshole?" I spewed. I wanted to beeline toward him and spit right in his face, but I was a lady. Staying tucked behind the kitchen counter, I glared at him. "Did you follow me here or something?"

Bryce grabbed at his stomach and snickered. "Follow you? Please don't flatter yourself. My article is about off-campus college landlords. Me and Mr. John have been working on it for weeks."

Fire burned in my belly and if it coursed through my body, I would surely erupt venom. "And that still doesn't explain

why your ass is *here*?" I made sure not to hide any of my contempt for Bryce. I respected him at work functions, but this
was personal, and he knew it.

"Don't you see, Indy. All college landlords have to register
with the school housing department, and I have been doing
walk-throughs of them all. The goal is to improve conditions
for off-campus housing. Someone included your dad's name
as a new landlord and so I came to check out the scene. I
called the number listed to schedule an appointment but no
one answered or called back. I was on this side of town and
decided to stop by. Now that I know you're connected to the
property, I'll make the story extra special. People would love
to hear about the water damage." He smiled wide and pointed
to the room's corner with a small, discolored hole.

Dad never answered the phone from unknown numbers
so if Bryce did call, Dad for sure wouldn't answer. Dad and
Chaquille had already tagged the water damage to be fixed in
the weeks to come. But Bryce would make sure people *knew*.
My dad completed most of the work himself. It wasn't finished,
but he made arrangements with the tenants to lower the rent
while he still made renovations. My dad said they agreed. It
was still livable, at least by my standards. Panic washed over
me as I bumrushed Bryce. Enough was enough. "Get the fuck
out of my house." I seethed. I was close to him now, in his
space, in his face.

Bryce took a step forward, unphased by my anger. His eyes
were dark and danced with excitement. "This is the problem
with you, Indy. You never want to do the work. It's always the
easy way out for you. That's why I pulled the plug on your article. Did you think I would let Harper put that trash on the
front? Not when I worked so hard on actual news. Meaningful
things that are important. You killed my Mr. Chestnut article,
but I won't let you kill this one."

My dad worked so hard on this house. Everything he did was for us, his family. Bryce would write a disparaging article about my dad and that would crush him and potentially ruin his chances of being the landlord that he wanted to be. Dad wasn't Bob the Builder. He did what he could, and between him and Chaquille, they did a decent enough job. How dare Bryce? The thought made me sick to my stomach, and I didn't want to think about what Dad would say when he saw his name and face plastered across *Synergy House News*. This type of press could ruin someone's future. Damn. Whenever my family took one step forward, they knocked us back three more.

Not today.

Bryce was right. I killed his Mr. Chestnut article. Just like I killed Mr. Chestnut. The buzz had died down and now Mr. Chestnut was barely a conversation anymore to anyone outside of the track team. Just like I was about to kill him. I looked Bryce up and down in disgust and saw a bulge in the front of his pants. His dick was hard while he planned my family's demise.

Pressing the keys into my hand, I flipped the top open to my pepper spray Ez insisted I carry.

Thank you, Ez.

"Bastard!" I screamed, and sprayed Bryce square in his face.

"Ugh! Ughh! You bitch!" He danced around the front room, rubbing at his eyes. He darted in the bathroom's direction, but I jumped in front of him, swung my knee back and kneed him right where his pants protruded.

Bryce lay writhing on the ground for the second time in months. This time, I wanted him to know exactly who and what I was. "How did that banana pudding taste?" I kneeled in front of him as he cried and rubbed at his eyes. He snorted and wheezed.

"You bitch! I'll kill you!" He coughed and grabbed at his balls. I hoped they were blue, green, and all different shades of *Indigo*.

I giggled at his pain. "Kill me? You don't even know—I'll kill you. Just like I killed Mr. Chestnut."

Bryce's eyes bugged out of his head, and he caught a second wind. "I should've known!" He grunted and lunged toward me. I scooched out of his grasp, but he caught the bottom of my jeans, yanked hard, and I tumbled on top of him. In a flash, he flipped over and kneeled on my legs. He slapped me in my face so hard it rang. He squeezed his hands around my neck until my eyes were blurry. His fingers pressed harder, and I gasped and scratched at his arms.

"That's right. You'll never beat me." Bryce whispered close to my face. We are nose to nose, and his rank breath made my eyes water.

"Indy?" Another voice cracked.

When I looked up, Will stood there, mouth gaped open, with a sachet of flowers in his hand.

CHAPTER THIRTY-FIVE

WILL TOOK TWO large steps and flew across the room. He yanked Bryce by the collar and shoved him off me. Will's leather jacket squeaked and pulled at his muscular arms. I saw just how good plumbing had been for his body. Will pummeled Bryce in the stomach over and over. He said one word.

"Indy." Punch. "Indy." Punch, punch. Bryce's stomach folded in like a slice of bread.

I scrambled to my feet; my heart somewhere in the pit of my belly. I gasped and brushed my braids out of my face. I was shaking. My arms and legs trembled like I was in the middle of Tennessee for New Year's Eve in a blizzard.

Bryce slid down the wall and blacked out.

Think, Indy, think. There was one thing I did and did well.

It involved water and sometimes fire. Sometimes both.

Racing to the bathroom, I turned on the tub of water and clogged up the drain. I dashed back into the living room, my shoes slipping and sliding under the newly waxed floor. Will leaned over the kitchen counter, taking deep breaths with his eyes squeezed shut.

"Indy," he whispered again.

"I know." I stood across from Will in the front room with Bryce slumped behind him. He ran his eyes up and down my body. He took in my newly braided hair, disheveled clothes, and crazed look.

"Indy." His eyes pleaded with me, trying to understand what he was seeing. His knuckles were red from Bryce's blood, and he was hunched over. None of it made sense, and I didn't have the words to explain it. Not now. Maybe not ever. Definitely not at this moment.

I had work to do.

Running behind Will, I pulled at Bryce's bruised arms. His bloody face was swollen to Texas sized proportions. "Umph! Umph!" I grunted. Bryce was stocky, and I was thankful Dad put in slick, laminate hardwood floors. They were easy to slide Bryce's heavy body into the bathroom.

Will said nothing and watched me while I pulled and tugged at Bryce, shimmying him down the hallway and carefully contorting his body to fit into the bathroom door. Will followed behind, watching my every move. I dropped to my knees and kneeled before Bryce. With my hands placed around his waist, I grunted and hoisted him up and he tumbled into the hot bath water. Bryce's eyes sprung open as the scorching water connected with his body.

"Ahhh!" he screamed. Holding him down, the water burned my hands, and I hissed at the pain. I jumped back, removed my hands, and slapped my foot into the hot water, trying to hold him down with my boot until he stopped moving. Bryce thrashed and clawed at my shoes. I grasped the walls, sliding under the wet floor and prayed he stayed down, and it was over quick. Will stood perfectly still; his eyes glued to me.

"Will!" I commanded.

He shook from his trance and blew out a loud breath. Moving from behind me, he kneeled next to the bathtub and placed his enormous arms into the water, holding Bryce down. Between my foot on his chest and Will's arms, Bryce flailed and gasped for breath. With each second passing, he took in larger gulps of water. His eyes were wide. So afraid. So clear. So angry. I wondered how long it took water to fill his lungs? How long did it take for someone to stop squirming and for the air to disappear out of their body? Bryce thrashed and shook under the scalding water. I winced under the heat. Sliding around the floor, how much more could I hold on? I panted. Me and Will stared each other down while we held Bryce down. Our eyes were locked. Soul ties between us.

Will held me down.

I remembered us in middle school and high school. Friend dates I took for granted when Will gave me lovey dovey eyes. Will joined the Newspaper Club when we were in high school, and he didn't know a lick about newspapers or writing.

He did it for me.

When Mom first went to Trochesse, I told Will I couldn't sleep at night. He snuck into my bedroom a few nights a week and held me tight as I slept. He snuck back out in the morning before the sun rose and made his way back across town to the big houses. We never talked about it—ever. I just knew to leave the window open, and he would be there. Quiet enough to comfort me and not wake Sidney.

Will was always there for me. Had always loved me in the shadows.

He stared back at me while we struggled to keep Bryce down. With love, questions, and confusion rolled into one face, which was so sexy and scary to me right now. What would he say? I was more exposed than I had ever been. What would he think of me?

With so many thoughts swarming in my mind, Bryce finally stopped squirming. His body shook and jerked before he released the grip he held on my shin under the water. Relief washed over me, and I fell back against the toilet and closed my eyes.

This was as far as my plan went. I wasn't sure what to do next.

CHAPTER THIRTY-SIX

WILL HUFFED AND puffed. Sweat littered his forehead. He closed his eyes and leaned against the tub. Almost as if he knew what I was thinking, he muttered, "Lie."

"Huh?" I gasped for air. "I didn't lie."

"No. Lye," he said and walked out of the bathroom.

I scrambled to my feet and followed him into the hallway as he darted across the floor, leaving water footprints. I watched from the window as Will popped the trunk to his car, and took out his plumber's bag, and another bag of tools. He held my stare and gazed at me through the window as he walked back in.

"I have Lye."

"What is that?" I questioned. My body went limp, scared of his answer.

"It's a chemical solution. We use it for clogged drains," he said. The large container jiggled, and he carried the solution jug with two handles. It had warning labels plastered around the outside. Will opened the container and I took a step forward and peered over the top.

"What's it smell like? And what does it do?" I asked, shuffling closer and raising an eyebrow.

"Actually, it smells like nothing. If we heat the tub with boiling water and keep it hot, we can pour this solution into the tub. In about four hours, his body will . . ." Will lifted his shoulders like I should already know what he's saying.

"What will happen?" I took a step back and paused. "We have to drain this water first, right?"

He nodded. "And once we drain and refill the tub with the solution, it will disintegrate his body. Into bones."

I gasp. "And you use this stuff for clogs?"

"Yeah, it's actually the best, but it's dangerous stuff. My instructor did an entire presentation on how to work with it. It will not be quick, and we have to keep the tub water hot." Will looked around the bathroom and eyed the sink. "That water won't be hot enough. We'll have to boil it. Are there any pots here?" Will darted to the kitchen.

"But won't the water turn cold? What do we do then." My mouth trembled.

"I guess we'll drain it every so often and refill it with boiling water. We have to do what we have to do, Indy."

The way he said my name made something in my pants tingle. My lips parted and I ran my tongue across my lips as I took stock of Will.

"I think Ms. Arletha bought some pots and pans and other kitchen stuff. Let me check," I said and dashed to the kitchen. Sure enough, there was a pot set sitting inside the dumbwaiter like it was waiting for me—brand new and shiny. I silently thank God himself for Ms. Arletha.

I grab the pots, fill them with water and turn on the stove. I heard a whooshing sound of water. When I poked my head into the bathroom, Will had poured the clear liquid into the

tub overtop of Bryce's body. He watched me, watching him. "The water is on." I whispered.

"Good," he said. "We'll need to keep the tub filled with boiling water for it to work best."

After a few minutes, the water boiled in each of the pots. Will and I removed the pots from the stove with brand-new oven mitts Ms. Arletha bought. We dumped the water into the bathtub. Yellow steam rose from the water.

Will and I slid down the walls, both of us sweating from the steamy bathroom. I sat next to the toilet, and he was across from me. "Indy." He drew in a sharp breath. "What happened here?"

I looked Will in the face and studied the man I knew so well. He thought he knew me too, but did he really? His skin was flushed, and he rested his hands on his knees. He sat in a casual, open stance. Unafraid of me.

I trusted him. I let him in. I was a killer. And that's what I told him.

Going back two years, I took a deep breath and started with Jaxon. Our agreement to write an article for him. Breaking my camera. Cutting my hair. Showing up at Dennis and Son's. Mr. Chestnut and Joya. Mr. Chestnut and the girls at school. Waking up to him in my dorm room. The dock in New Orleans. The water below.

Will listened. He closed his eyes and laid his head against the wall when I explained where I had just come from the night we were in the hotel after I left Mr. Chestnut and the other man at the bottom of the lake.

The night I chose Chaquille.

I didn't tell him about the other man I killed. Not that he wasn't important. He was another life that I took and added to my body count, but right now—he didn't matter to *this* story. I fumbled with my words, telling Will every sorted detail that I could think of. Tears clouded my vision and my anger bubbled as I recalled how men really had tried me over and over and the depths that I had let them take me.

I was not the one to play with.

When I got to Bryce, my voice cracked when I recalled banana pudding, and him deleting the article from my computer. The slights. The jabs. The shade. I was inflamed with hatred for what my life turned into. Most people go to college and reminisce about how they found themselves and their life purpose. This was where they became adults. Some found college sweethearts, built careers and made connections that would last them a lifetime. I struggled to stay afloat, fight off voices, and still managed to collect body after body—now year after year. I was expecting my college years to be something like my favorite show, *A Different World*. And it was.

College was different world from Tunica Rivers. But yet— the same.

And what was worse? Sometimes I liked the feeling. It brought a rush of emotions. Theodora told me when she was sitting in class, her mind would drift to Dylan. She jumped in her seat and looked around, wondering if anyone knew she was having sex flashbacks. She smiled and asked if that ever happened to me. I nodded, only I didn't recall sex flashbacks. I recalled murder flashbacks, and that was the biggest turn on for me. A shot of dopamine, or, however, Ms. Ramos had explained, made me fantasize and bite down on my pen in class at the memories.

Angry tears continued to fall and my coochie throbbed as I watched Will lick his lips and decipher my words. He. Looked. So. Good.

What a mess I was. What a mess.

"Indy. You've been dealing with all of this, and you haven't told anyone?" Will gazed at me.

Lowering my head. I grimaced. "No one knows everything. Not like you."

Will said nothing about what I said and every thirty minutes for the next four hours, Will and I re-filled the pots with more hot water, so it stayed scalding. I slugged back and forth to the tub, emptying water, refilling the tub, adding more Lye, and checking the time. I was tired and judging by Will's heavy eyes—so was he.

"Do you remember that time we were in middle school, and we accidentally locked ourselves in the freezer in the Home Economics room?" Will recalled.

A throaty laugh escaped me. "Of course! We were only in there about an hour, but it felt so long! I really thought we would be frozen alive!"

"Me too! Locked in a freezer. We were so young, man. Kids." Will reminisced. His hand brushed my knee. He was in front of me in the bathroom on the floor. "I'm still not sure how that door locked behind us and no one knew we were in there!"

I snorted and closed my dropping eyes.

Minutes later, Will nudged me. "Indy. Wake up. Look," he said.

Wiping my eyes, I peered over the bathtub ledge. "Oh, shit."

Bryce was no more. The water was a murky brown color that looked like light roast coffee. His body was disintegrated, and all that was left were bones.

CHAPTER THIRTY-SEVEN

"WHAT NOW?" I mumbled. It. worked. It. Really. Worked.

"I have an idea. We can just drain the tub. The solution at this point is only water, salt, and other chemicals that are safe to go down the drain. Can you throw the bones in water, somewhere? Like a lake or something? We have to get rid of them."

I paused. There was a small lake about thirty minutes from here. Checking the time, it was after midnight and dark. Good. I could take the bones and dump them straight into the water, hopefully with no one seeing.

"What about his car?" I whispered and turned toward the front window with his ride out front.

"I'm not sure about that one, Indy. I can drive it somewhere. But I'm sure they would sweep it and find DNA."

Will and I were quiet for a moment, pondering what to do. "How about. . . no. That won't work." I frowned.

"What?" Will questioned.

"I'll write a letter. I'll have Bryce confess to the murder of Mr. Chestnut. Make it seem like he did it, and that's why he was so adamant about running the story. So he could stay involved."

"And the car?" Will's face was tight and ashen.

"We can leave it at Synergy House. They don't have cameras outside or inside."

And I would know. When my article went missing, I asked security if there were any cameras so I could focus them on my desk. They laughed and said, *'Miss Lady, they barely pay us a decent salary. Do you think they have cameras outside this building, let alone inside?'*

"And where is his cell phone? Will they track it to the house?" Will quizzed.

He was good. Too good at this. How did he know just what to ask? Grateful was an understatement right now.

"Bryce bragged about turning off the GPS on his phone. Said an ex used it to track him and he keeps it off ever since then." I recollected his pompous story.

"Are you sure? Where is it?"

"No. I'm not sure, but that's what he said. He left the phone in the car."

"Okay. . . Okay . . ." Will takes a deep breath and wipes his brow. "I guess we'll just have to pray."

It seemed a little obnoxious, to pray in this moment after killing a man. But I squeezed my eyes shut anyway and grabbed Will's hands. Will and I did the most toxic shit ever—and we prayed to God that Bryce's phone wouldn't be tracked. I prayed to Mom, Ez, and Mama Jackie too.

"Now you go, take his car to Synergy House. Let it sit there. Write something in his notebook. Maybe even Mr. Chestnut's name over and over. Like he was obsessed, or something. Indy. Try to match his handwriting." Will instructed. "I'll finish up here and get everything cleaned up. And then, Indy? We don't speak of this ever again."

I nodded and listened to Will—my protector. My savior. I hung to his every word with wide eyes.

"Indy. You can do this. You always could." Will stood in front of me and moved in close. I inhaled his cologne, and the smell sent fire to my loins. I took some toilet paper and patted Will's wet forehead. "I love you, Indy. I'll always love you."

"What about Ashli?"

"What about Chaquille?"

I didn't have an answer for him, and so I said nothing except for more of the truth. "I love you too." My lips parted and brushed his.

"We're locked in now. You and me. Locked in, Indy."

"Locked in," I repeated.

CHAPTER THIRTY-EIGHT

NAOMI READ THE head-line out loud. "'*Missing student leaves confession note to track coach's murder.*' What is going on at Titus University?" she exclaimed.

Chomping down on my cheeseburger, I shook my head. "I know, right?"

"So, you're not in the least bit worried that a man you work with has randomly disappeared and claims to have killed the same person who he was writing an exposé about? The same man from your hometown?" Theodora frowned.

Swallowing my last chew, it went down dry. Theodora wanted to challenge everything these days, and she was turning into our resident Olivia Pope with the way she defended Mr. Chestnut and Bryce. "What am I supposed to do, Theodora?"

Theodora pushed her tray away from the table. "I just find it weird. I saw him two weeks ago, and he was excited about his story about Mr. Chestnut. He said it was received well and he really thought someone would take a further look into the disappearance. And now Bryce has disappeared? Makes little sense to me." Theodora pushed french fries around on her tray.

One week. It took one full week for Synergy House to realize that Bryce's absences coupled with his car sitting outside in the parking lot and not moving meant shady business. By that time, Will and I had cleaned up the house and disposed of bones. The tenants moved in and no one was the wiser.

"It's terrible. You're right though. What is happening at Titus?" I shook my head. Mr. John called a staff meeting yesterday and finally admitted to the secret article about *"Lemon Landlords"* he called it. He said they were planning to set up an anonymous tip line for people to call in and report shady landlords in hopes to improve off campus living concerns. Bryce was investigating each of them. Mr. John gave us and the police searching for Bryce, a list of the properties he was researching. I smiled when I didn't see Dad's name. Bryce said they added it late. New rules were enacted, and effective immediately—all staff members at Synergy House who went out into the field for assignments were given work cell phones and required to have them turned on at all times.

There was no trace of Bryce, me, Dad, or his property. The police interviewed everyone at Synergy House but with no video or photo evidence, and nothing found on the phone, they were turning up less and less leads. Good.

After Bryce's disappearance they *found* money for cameras inside and outside Synergy House. The place was lit up like Times Square now. Too bad they didn't have them when my article went missing.

I was sure they swept his car for fingerprints and clues. When I drove it to Synergy House, I was careful to wear gloves that Will had in his plumber's bag. Bryce had a jacket sitting in his front seat and I pulled it on and wore it all the way to Synergy House and prayed whatever DNA they found in the car belonged to him and this jacket.

No one came banging down my door yet.

Prayers answered.

My phone chimed, and when I looked down, it was Will. I knew it was him before I even checked. He texted me every day during his lunch break at noon. He sent heart eye emojis.

My stomach fluttered, and I sent them back to him.

I brushed my fingers against the dog tags circling my neck, and my shifty love did somersaults at the thought of Chaquille. Was it possible to be in love with two men at the same time? I was, I realized. I really was. And they both loved me too. The shit felt like glass digging into my arms. It was painful and confusing. Then sometimes it felt like I was on a high, gliding through the air. Or at an amusement park, zipping back and forth fast. So fast that I don't know if I'm coming or going. I'm whipping up, down, side to side, and I'm laughing because I'm scared but it's fun.

And the voices. The entire night I was with Will handling Bryce, they didn't say a word. Every other time I had killed, they guided me along the way. This time, I did it on my own. Albeit, Will was there—my thoughts were my own.

Once again, prayer worked. And maybe medication, too.

"Do you want any of this burger?" I held up my tray to Naomi.

"Eww, I'm giving up red meat. Me and Ivelisse watched a special about how it's farmed on Netflix." She shuddered and waved me away. "No, I'm good."

"Fine," I giggled, and stuffed the last few pickles in my mouth. The burger was so tasty. I was ravenous these days after taking out Bryce.

Theodora squinted at me with a puzzled look on her face.

Probably wondering who I was.

Fuck around and find out.

NOT THE END

WANT TO READ MORE?
CHECK OUT OTHER LITERARY
WORKS BY JANAY HARDEN

Hey, Brown Girl

Forty-two Minutes: Book 1 of the Indigo Lewis Series

Someone More Like Myself: Book 2 of the Indigo Lewis Series

April Showers
Coming Soon Summer 2023

Signup at the QR code link below for more information!

www.naywrites.com